THE
UNWANTED
INHERITANCE
OF THE
BOOKMAN
BROTHERS

a novella by
Tammie Painter

The Unwanted Inheritance of the Bookman Brothers

First Edition, February 2023
also available as an ebook

You may contact the author by email at
Tammie@tammiepainter.com
Mailing Address:
Daisy Dog Media
P.O. Box 165
Netarts, Oregon 97143, USA

ALSO BY TAMMIE PAINTER

WHAT READERS HAVE TO SAY ABOUT TAMMIE PAINTER'S BOOKS

THE CASSIE BLACK TRILOGY...

...suffused with dark humor and witty dialogue, of the sort that Painter excels at...a fun read for anyone who enjoys fast-paced, somewhat snarky, somewhat twisted, fantasy adventures.
—Berthold Gambrel, author of *Vespasian Moon's Fabulous Autumn Carnival*

...a fun and entertaining read. Great wit too.
—Carrie Rubin, author of *The Bone Curse*

Wow and wow again! I absolutely loved this book! ...you don't want to put it down.
—Goodreads Reviewer

I was unable to put this down when I started reading it. The author combines humour with a fast paced murder mystery all packed into a funeral home.
—Amazon Reviewer

A wonderful surprise greeted me with an entertaining story that was written with humor, a great story line and new twist on the undead.
—J. Tate, Eugene Reviewer

THE CIRCUS OF UNUSUAL CREATURES MYSTERIES

The series keeps getting better.
—Bookbub Reviewer

Very funny and laughs out loud will be heard when reading it...this was so good l read it in one sitting couldn't put it down
—Goodreads Reviewer

What a stunning sequel! This was a charming tale of dragons, deception, and dastardly deeds, and I loved every minute of it.
—Jonathan Pongratz, author of Reaper

What a truly FUN, lighthearted read, full of fantastical and lovable characters! ...intricately woven with twists and kept me guessing until the very end.
—Goodreads Reviewer

What fun!
—Sarah Angleton, author of White Man's Graveyard

...lots of humour, characters with depth, and a good fun romp...an easy, fun read, packed with fascinating details of the new world she's created.
—Kim M. Watt, author of Baking Bad

*To everyone who believes in
the magic of books.*

THE UNWANTED INHERITANCE OF THE BOOKMAN BROTHERS

CHAPTER ONE

A good bookshop is just a genteel Black
Hole that knows how to read.

—Terry Pratchett

"I, Gerald Bookman, being of sound mind and
body—"

At the scoffing sound from her audience of
two, the lawyer stopped reading and peered over
her rimless spectacles. She arched an eyebrow
that had stubbornly remained black even after the
rest of her hair had gone grey years ago.

With schoolboy-like guilt on their faces, the
two men shifted in their seats to sit up straighter.
The lawyer's gaze drifted back to the will.

"—have decreed the distribution of my worldly
goods as set forth..."

The brothers, twins who were in no way
identical, leaned forward. The lawyer could
almost hear them salivating and wondered if she
shouldn't have suggested quick-drying carpet

when the firm redecorated last spring.

"My clothes shall go to the Sunny Second Chances Charity Shop. All except for my collection of Christmas sweaters that I wish to be passed on to Rafi Nazzar, a devoted customer who always admired them, and my socks which I'd like—"

"Sorry, but do we have to listen to all this? You know, the parts that don't pertain to us?" asked Enton Bookman, a rail-thin beanpole of a man whose shaggy hair looked like it had frightened off the last comb that dared come near it.

"Yeah, not to be rude, but we've got plans," declared Reggie, who, although shorter than his twin, had apparently nabbed all the muscle cells when the two shared a womb. It took every bit of the lawyer's self-control not to stare at his oddly bulbous forehead when he spoke.

The lawyer glanced reproachfully from one brother to the other. Normally, when someone asked her to "get to the good part," she refused to comply. These were the final wishes of a loved one, after all. Their last concerns, hopes, and thoughts beyond what had been uttered on their deathbed. Was it so difficult to listen to these words in their entirety?

The lawyer's specialty was contract law, but the senior partner occasionally assigned her estate cases. And in her experience, these requests to "hurry up" were never made by people whose dearly departed hadn't been wealthy. People from families of average means knew they weren't getting much and so endured the ritual of the full reading.

No, it was only when someone with an impressive collection of assets died that this air of urgency, of impatience, of naked want filled her office. Delayed gratification meant nothing to the greedy. Especially the greedy who might be a few short paragraphs away from a financial windfall.

But it was Friday of a holiday weekend. The lawyer had booked a vacation rental on the Coast, and she was desperate to flee the office early to get started on the two-hour drive west before the majority of Portlanders began chugging toward the beach and clogging the highways. Her eyes flicked to the clock on her desk. Only a few minutes after one o'clock. There'd be no traffic if she wrapped this up quickly. The lawyer scanned down Gerald Bookman's will to find the section that would most interest her audience.

"To my grandsons, Reggie and Enton, your parents didn't leave you much at their untimely passing. So, as I have always done, I would like to ensure you have a place you can call your own for the rest of your days."

Both twins, who again had started slouching, suddenly found their backbones eager to hold their bodies fully upright. They leaned in, eyes wide.

The lawyer wondered if they were expecting to inherit Mr Bookman's home. She'd seen the appraiser's detail sheet on the three-bedroom bungalow in Lake Oswego — a suburb south of Portland where even a fixer-upper could set you back half a million. She bit her lip to keep from laughing at the men's misguided fervor. She knew it was devilish of her, but she simply had to see their reaction to the will's actual contents. She continued from memory to keep an eye on their faces.

"This is why I leave to you my shop, Bookman's Bookstore. Because wherever there are books, there is a home."

As she knew it would, the news did not cause the men to erupt with cheers and hoots of delight like someone winning the jackpot. Instead, the news was followed by a duet of dissatisfied groans and the creaking of chairs as their spines, weakened by the letdown, slumped once more.

"You're disappointed?" she asked. She couldn't understand why. The bookshop, only a few blocks away from the law office, was an established business in Sellwood — a perpetually trendy shopping, dining, and residential area of Portland. The property alone would set the twins up for an easy life.

"Gramps had money enough for nice vacations and a decent house. Where's that going, then?" Reggie asked accusingly.

The lawyer, although she knew the answer, and although she was keen to get out of town, pretended to peruse the papers in front of her. She ran her index finger along the will's numbered lines, then tapped the sheet when she found the one she'd been after. Again, she forced back the grin that was twitching at the corners of her lips.

"My home shall be sold. After paying off the small amount of my remaining medical expenses and my lawyer's fees, the profits along with whatever is in my savings account shall be evenly split between the library systems of the greater Portland area and the Meow Meow Cat Rescue."

"That's all we get? A bookshop?" Enton asked, more dumbstruck than angry.

"We don't even like books," Reggie declared, as if this were something to be proud of.

"Yes, well, that comes as no surprise," the lawyer said before she could stop herself. She spoke quickly to cover up her momentary slip of unprofessionalism. "Look—" Her attention darted again to the desk clock, a gift from the partners for her fifteen-year anniversary. No doubt to remind her about those all-important billable hours. If she didn't get on the road in the next fifteen minutes, she'd be yet another slow-moving cog in Highway 26's bumper-to-bumper traffic. "You won't be able to do anything with the long weekend coming. Have a think about it. You can collect the keys now to look the property over, then I'll be in touch early next week with the title and business license transfer."

"We don't want anything to do with it," Reggie said without consulting his lanky brother. "Place is nothing to us."

"Right," the lawyer said waspishly. She knocked the papers against her desk to straighten them and to signal time was up. "Like I said, check the place out and give it a think over the weekend. Who knows, you might change your minds. Perhaps you'll discover you want to get involved in the book trade."

"We won't," Reggie insisted.

"Yes, well, that's your decision. Now, as I've got to get on the road…"

She closed the manila file labeled *Bookman* and stood. The men, as if marionettes joined to the same string, popped out of their seats the instant she did. The lawyer bid the brothers a safe holiday and shook their hands farewell.

As soon as they turned to go, she wiped their clammy sweat from her palm, then noted the time for billing.

CHAPTER TWO

Happiness. That's what books smell like…
That's why I always wanted to have a
bookshop. What better life than to trade in
happiness?

—Sarah MacLean, The Rogue Not Taken

Outside of the law office, the bewildered brothers sat in their car, a Civic that had seen its best days sometime around the second term of Clinton's presidency. As Reggie stared at the keys the lawyer's assistant had handed him on their way out, a dark-haired girl skipped by, clutching a trio of books to her chest. When she stepped into the crosswalk, she caught Enton's eye and grinned. Not in the way of a kid, at least no kid Enton had ever encountered, but in the way of a cunning adult who knew more than you ever will.

"Who the hell skips these days?" Enton muttered, and Reggie looked up from the keys.

"Skipping?" Reggie asked.

Just then, the light changed and a van emblazoned with bright, primary colors and the words *Sunny Second Chances Charity Shop* in a jaunty font came to a halt beside the Civic, blocking Enton's view of the girl.

"Never mind. What are we going to do with a bookstore?" Enton asked for the third time — the first two times having elicited no response from his twin.

"How the hell should I know?"

When the light changed, a station wagon followed along behind the charity van. Stuck crookedly to the car's side panel was a decal declaring, "We buy houses. Cash. Any condition. Money today!" above a number that wasn't local.

Reggie clapped his meaty hands together, startling Enton, who'd been peering across the street to see where the girl had gone.

"It's obvious, right? We sell the shop. Just think about it. This neighborhood is hopping, and Gramps's place is on prime real estate that's gotta be big enough for a small apartment building or a couple townhouses. A real estate developer. That's what we need."

"Well, you're not going to find one on a holiday weekend."

"Yeah, probably lounging in some resort they just built. Lucky bastards."

"How much you think we might get? Six hundred thousand?"

"Enton," Reggie said in that condescending way he had, as if just because he was three minutes older, he was three decades wiser.

"Seven hundred thousand?" Enton guessed.

"There are rundown, one-bedroom shacks going for that much in Sellwood. We could get, I don't know, at a conservative guess, three million for it."

"Three million?" Enton repeated, sitting up taller and looking at the shop's keys as if they'd suddenly become holy relics. "You serious?"

"It's just a guess, but yeah. Close to that, anyway."

"We'd be set for life. That trip we got planned—" Because the brothers, after scrimping and saving for two years, hoped to book themselves a two-week vacation to France. A hope neither of them truly believed would ever happen. Until now. "We could go business class."

"Enton, if we can close up that shop and get the deal done in time, we're going first class." Reggie smiled and got a dreamy look in his eye. "We'll hang out in the VIP lounge before boarding, drink free-flowing champagne the entire flight, upgrade our rooms to suites, and hire private tour guides. What do you say we go look at our little book-filled bonanza?"

"I thought it was called— Oh, I get it," Enton said with a wink. He didn't really get it, but, sensing Reggie's derision hovering just behind his euphoria, knew better than to admit his ignorance.

* * *

"Welcome to Bookman's Bookshop," the clerk trilled, practically singing along with the bell above the door when Reggie and Enton stepped in.

"You're open?" asked Reggie.

"Six days a week," the clerk replied brightly, and Enton wondered how much coffee this guy was consuming. "Closed Mondays. As well as Christmas, New Year's, and Thanksgiving, of course."

"Not for the death of the store owner?" Reggie asked critically.

Blinking his long-lashed, mischievous eyes and swallowing hard as if fighting back emotion, the clerk said, "He told us not to. Mr B said getting books into people's hands was more important than moping over him."

A small, elderly woman wearing a bright pink rain jacket set a pile of books on the counter. The clerk raised his finger to the brothers in a just-a-moment gesture. Reggie gave a disgruntled sigh and crossed his arms over his chest. Enton took the chance to glance around.

He hadn't been in the shop since he was a teenager, but it was the exact same as he'd remembered it. The cash register desk sat in a direct line to the door. From there, the bookshop sprawled out across a vast space, divided into sections, not by walls, but by cherrywood bookshelves. Heading straight back, brought you to a set of stairs that led up to Gramps's office, a break room, a walkway from which you could view the entire retail floor, and an access panel to the attic that Reggie, for all his tough-guy act, could never muster the courage to enter.

"This all for today, Mrs O'Reilly?"

"Yes, these should see me through for a few days. Such good company they are."

The clerk pushed forward a book that had been by the till and tapped his index finger on the cover. Enton could just make out a muscular man in period costume clutching a gasping woman. "Especially this series?"

The woman smiled and playfully slapped the clerk's hand. "You! Always trying to sneak that one in."

"I'm just saying, you might like it. It's," he

paused, "historically accurate."

"Fine," the woman said, her eyes glinting with warm amusement. "I'll take it, but only to get you to stop pestering me."

"Terrific. Then that'll be five dollars and ninety-five cents, Mrs O'Reilly."

"Five ninety-five?" Reggie blurted. "The woman brought up four books, and you just biggie-sized her to five. That's got to be more than five freaking ninety-five."

The woman gaped at Reggie and gripped more tightly to her purse.

"You're absolutely right," said the clerk in a sweet, yet challenging manner. "You forgot your punch card, Mrs O'Reilly. You're due a free book. And since this one was my recommendation, it's Bookman policy not to charge you for it. So that—" he tapped a few keys on the register "—brings us to three dollars and ninety-six cents."

Keeping one eye on Reggie, Mrs O'Reilly dipped her hand as quickly as possible into her bag, then into a coin purse. She pulled out a five-dollar bill and didn't let it go until it was safely in the clerk's hand.

"Please keep the change," she told him.

"I'll add it to your store credit."

"You're making Mr Bookman proud, Sebastian. So proud," she added with a sniffle. She took the tissue the clerk offered, collected her bag of books, and left the shop, but not before giving the twins a scathing look.

"Now," said the clerk, "may I help you two? Perhaps the self-help section? Or I believe we have a collection of Miss Manners' articles you might like."

"Do you know who we are?"

"I'd say Tweedle Dee and Tweedle Dumb, but they were far less rude."

"We," said Reggie, placing both hands on the cashier's desk and looming forward, "are your new bosses. We've inherited this shop, and if you keep giving away our profits, we're going to have to have a little chat."

"So you're the grandsons," Sebastian said, completely unperturbed by Reggie's play of aggression. He then darted a glance to his left where a framed photo hung on the wall. It was of the brothers, aged perhaps six years old, in the children's section of the bookstore. Each boy held a large book with cartoonish covers, and each wore smiles of delight as they peered out from a fort made of dictionaries, atlases, and encyclopedias. The photo's wooden frame had been carved to look like books on a shelf, and on its lower portion were the words, "Build a world of books."

"Yes, I'm Enton and this is Reggie." Enton stuck out his hand in a gesture of friendship. "Pleased to—"

Reggie knocked Enton's outstretched hand aside, as if Enton were a child reaching for a poisonous plant.

"Pleased to let you know," said Reggie, "that once you finish up for the day, you may go home."

"Yes, that is what I normally do at the end of the day," Sebastian said wryly.

"No, I mean, for the weekend," said Reggie, flustered by the clerk's scurrilously arched eyebrows and calm demeanor. "For good. This is the shop's final day."

"Final day? But—" Sebastian, finally thrown off his stride, stumbled over his words. "We've got new books coming out Tuesday, and holiday weekends are always a favorite with shoppers."

"Well, not this holiday," said Enton with a confident nod. "We're going to be millionaires and fly first class."

"Right, but you do know people love this place. It's an institution."

Reggie pondered this a moment. The shop was in good shape. Windows clean, shelves straight, floor polished, landscaping out front tidy. The place wasn't shabbily kept or a haphazard mess like some used bookstores. Even if old ladies got free romance novels on occasion, Bookman's

Bookshop must be making a good profit. Maybe they shouldn't be so quick to sell.

"I need to see the accounts books," Reggie stated.

"Right this way," the clerk said, then led them through the shop. People milled about, chatting and browsing, and Sebastian greeted nearly all of them by name. He guided the brothers toward a section to which a non-fiction sign pointed, then zigzagged his way through a few shelves until he stopped at one labeled Basic Bookkeeping.

Reggie scowled at the dark-haired pest.

"I meant the store's records of expenses, income, and the like. Never mind. I remember where Gramps's office is." From the front, the entry bell chimed. "You best get back to your post. And no more freebies."

"It's Bookman policy," Sebastian said with cheery defiance before flouncing away.

"What do you wanna see the accounts for?" asked Enton. "We don't need to see them to sell the place, do we?"

"I'm just wondering what the profit margin is," Reggie said, swiping his finger along the gleaming banister as they headed up the stairs to the shop's second level. He inspected the finger and found not a speck of dust. "This place looks like it's doing pretty well."

"But the champagne."

"You've gotta think long-term, Enton. If this place is doing as well as it looks," he said, pointing over the railing to the shop below. It was busy with customers, most of whom carried baskets brimming with books. "If we got someone, not that twat at the register, to manage it, we could have an easy flow of cash without any work."

Enton didn't like the sound of that, but the sight of what — or rather who — was below stopped him from commenting.

"There's that girl again," he said.

"What girl?" Reggie grumbled, not bothering to look back as he turned the knob of the office door. It wasn't even locked. What kind of trusting fool had their grandfather been?

"The one— Oh, maybe you didn't see her. Went skipping past the car with a bunch of books."

"Keep an eye on her. She might be stealing them. Why else would a kid be in a bookshop?"

"Can I look over the accounts with you?"

"Better not. You're terrible at math," Reggie said, and slammed the door on his brother.

CHAPTER THREE

Books and doors are the same thing. You
open them, and you go through into
another world.

—Jeanette Winterson

When Reggie had slammed the door on his
brother, Enton had startled and ended up losing
sight of the girl. Now, Enton leaned on the
banister to watch the shop activity below.

Some customers had a lackadaisical air. They'd
stroll amongst the stacks, scanning the shelves
seemingly unconcerned with what they were
passing. Then they'd suddenly come to a stop,
pull a book from a shelf, and drop it into their
basket with a satisfied smile on their lips and
without ever opening the cover.

Other shoppers seemed on a mission and
would carefully look over each spine in the
section they'd made a beeline for. They gave their
final treasures a tad more scrutiny, but in every

case, the book would eventually pass muster and be taken up to the till for purchase.

Enton was especially interested in the surprising number of people pointing out books to perfect strangers, or even taking them — by the hand in one case — to an entirely different section of the store to show them a book. In almost every case, the shopper would add that shown book to their basket.

As Reggie remained sequestered behind the office door, Enton caught sight of Sebastian carrying a box of books. Books that he shelved with hardly a glance at the spines. Even books with tattered covers were tossed onto a shelf, and Enton wondered about the quality of Bookman's inventory.

Sebastian was down to his last few books when a man came up to him and asked something. The clerk nodded, reached into the box, and handed the man an age-stained, dog-eared paperback. Enton expected the man to reject it. After all, the thing looked like it might fall apart the minute the cover was peeled back. But when the man took it in his hand, Enton had to rub his eyes.

He tried to tell himself it hadn't happened, that perhaps there'd been a trick of the light, but as his vision refocussed, the scene was the same.

But the book wasn't. The book had definitely changed. In the customer's hand, the formerly ratty paperback could now pass for a new release hot off the presses.

Enton blinked, then glanced at his watch. That had to be it. It was well past his normal lunchtime and he never did feel right when he got hungry. Before he could resume his people watching, the office door opened.

"Reggie, you're not gonna believe this—"

"Does it have to do with the shop?"

"Yeah. See, I just—"

"Save it. This place ain't worth the bricks it's built with. I don't know what tricks he was pulling, but there's no legal way Gramps could have afforded to keep this place afloat."

"Did he owe money?" Enton asked, picturing the three million vanishing like the bubbles in a flute of champagne. From what he could see below, the secondhand book business was booming. Then again, if Gramps had had a gambling problem, that might explain whatever discrepancies Reggie had found.

Or, he thought as Sebastian looked up and gave him a knowing grin, perhaps a certain clerk was pilfering from the cash drawer.

"No. Gramps's books are perfectly even. He's got no real outstanding debt. Just this year's taxes, that sort of thing. He paid himself a small salary, barely enough to get by, if you ask me, but all the rest of his income perfectly balances with expenses."

"That's good, isn't it?"

"For him, not for us. I don't get how he afforded that house of his or those vacations he took, but we ain't keeping this place. Ain't worth it. Soon as this weekend's over, we're finding a developer and seeing what they've got to say."

"So we're back to first class?"

"First class all the way," Reggie said, companionably wrapping a heavy arm over his brother's shoulder.

Chapter Four

That's the thing about books. They let you travel without moving your feet.

—Jhumpa Lahiri

The brothers trudged back down the stairs and meandered their way past the people roaming amongst the shop's shelves. At the cashier's desk. six customers were queued up — each of them ready to fork over (until Sebastian gave them their loyalty discount) at least five bucks each.

How was the shop not turning a hefty profit? It boggled Reggie's calculating mind. Just as he reached the door, over which hung a sign stating, '*Books are magic*,' he turned and addressed the people in line.

"Buy what you can, everyone. Today is the last day the doors to this waste of real estate will be open for business."

Enton smiled apologetically to the group. Some of them were glowering at his loudmouthed twin who was already striding out the door, while others whispered speculatively to their in-line neighbor. As Enton passed under the sign and stepped across the store's threshold, he heard Sebastian saying, "New owner, great sense of humor," to many a relieved sigh.

* * *

The next day, to Enton's confusion and surprise, Reggie suggested they go to the bookshop.

"But I was going to tackle that spot in the ceiling today," said Enton.

Because even a decade after Gramps had helped them buy it, the brothers' home remained a fixer-upper. Amongst a myriad of other repairs the house needed, the roof above Reggie's bedroom leaked. Reggie's solution had been to put a bucket under the drip. He then failed to empty the bucket when it overflowed during a rainstorm. Since Reggie's room was located just above the kitchen, a portion of the kitchen ceiling now sagged like the back of an overworked mule. Enton was no Mr Fix-It, but he was determined to repair both the leak and the sag while the weather was dry.

But Reggie insisted they had to go and grabbed the car keys off the battered, formica-topped dining table.

"We need to get a handle on that stock. I'm betting some of those newer books can be sent back to the publisher for a refund. Others, who knows, there's gotta be a few rare editions that might be worth a bundle."

Enton thought of the tattered book he'd seen the day before as he followed his twin out to the driveway.

"Reggie, can a book change its appearance?" he asked, sliding into the passenger seat after fighting with the dented door of their hatchback.

"What in the world of purple unicorns are you talking about?" Reggie asked as he turned the key in the ignition. Something under the hood made a grinding sound for a good fifteen seconds before the engine finally sputtered to life.

"Like a book looking ready for the bin, then it looks brand new. You ever hear about that?"

"There's book restorers, sure." Reggie backed out of the driveway. Then, as the gears squealed their way out of reverse, he slammed on the brakes. "Damn it!"

Reggie smashed his hand against the steering wheel. The horn blared. Enton stared through the windshield, his heart throbbing like an unbalanced helicopter rotor. It was the dark-haired girl, this time pulling a royal blue wagon that contained about a dozen books. She smiled at the brothers as she skipped along, the wagon clattering behind her.

"What's with kids these days?" griped Reggie, who didn't recognize the girl from the previous day. "We ever step out in front of a moving vehicle like that? No. Now these entitled brats think the world is supposed to stop for them." Reggie complained about the state of child-rearing as his angry grip on the steering wheel made for a jerky three-mile drive to Bookman's Bookshop.

"And just what the hell is *he* doing here?" Reggie hurled himself out of the car, flinging the much-abused car door shut. "I told you to stay home. We're closed."

Enton got out and nodded a greeting to Sebastian, who was waiting by the shop's door.

"I have personal items to collect."

"And you couldn't have taken them with you yesterday?" Reggie asked as he yanked down and wadded up a Save Our Shop flyer someone had taped to the window. Then another, and another.

"Forgot a couple things. It's hard to believe how many personal items you end up collecting when you've worked so long at a place." Enton scrutinized Sebastian's face. There wasn't a single wrinkle, not even the faintest toe of crow's feet. Enton guessed the clerk might be twenty-two, twenty-five at the most. How long could he have possibly worked for Gramps? "Plus, we never discussed my severance package."

Reggie had just pushed the shop door open when Sebastian said this. The entry bell chimed like a punctuation mark.

"Your what?" Reggie asked.

"Severance package. Compensation for the job you've suddenly booted me out of. It's in my contract."

"A contract a dead man agreed to, not me."

"Actually," said a woman, striding up to the trio of men, "as you've inherited the shop, you are legally bound to any employee agreements or other business contracts your grandfather signed. Of course, if you'd like to change them, I'd be glad to offer my services."

Enton shook the lawyer's hand, then gestured her and Sebastian inside.

"What are you doing here?" Reggie asked accusingly. "We're not being billed for your time, are we? I mean, we didn't schedule this meeting. And don't you take nothing that don't belong to you," he shouted at Sebastian, who was already heading toward the upstairs break room.

"No, I won't be billing for this, but you may want to make an appointment for another consultation with me. There seems to be an unexpected—"

"Oy! You can't be in here. We're closed."

The dark-haired girl smiled at Reggie as if he were simply not getting a joke she'd already had to explain three times. Enton checked outside and saw the blue wagon parked near the door. It was now empty of books.

"Sabrina, that you?" called Sebastian, peering down from the walkway. "Come up and help." To the three questioning faces below, he added, "Sabrina's my sister."

"I don't care if she's the Queen of Egypt. She can't be in here," Reggie blustered, but the girl skipped past him and up the stairs to her brother.

"Mr Bookman," said the lawyer insistently, "if you don't pay attention, I will indeed start tallying up these very billable minutes."

"How was your trip?" Enton asked, having just remembered her desire to get out of town.

"Non-existent. Apparently, the last guest at the vacation rental I'd reserved had the bright idea to deep-fry an entire chicken. Unfortunately, their definition of *deep-frying* meant pouring hot peanut oil over the chicken as it sat on the barbecue. The barbecue they'd moved indoors since it was threatening to rain. The rental was ruined, the owner hadn't bothered to tell me, every hotel was booked solid because of the holiday, so I turned around and drove straight back home."

"Well, the traffic must have been light on the return trip," Enton said.

"Who cares?" Reggie interrupted. "What are you here for? Since I'm sure it's not to regale us with your weekend woes."

The lawyer stared at Reggie a moment, then reached into the leather satchel she had slung over her shoulder. She pulled out a manila envelope and held it up.

"As I was trying to say, there's been some unexpected complications. From rumors racing around the neighborhood, I'm guessing you still want to sell this place?"

"Of course. It's easy money," Reggie said confidently, but in his mind's eye, Enton saw the cork being crammed back into his bottle of free-flowing champagne.

"Well, then you better turn that closed sign to open."

The lawyer slapped the envelope into Reggie's palm.

"Mind explaining?"

"Your grandfather wrote up his original will with the senior partner of my firm, who only recently passed the case on to me. The will I read was merely the distribution of assets. I thought it was complete, but right when I was discovering the state of my vacation rental yesterday, my paralegal texted me to point out I had missed a key clause, a contingency in the senior partner's version of the will. Really, contract law is my strong suit, not estate law, so I failed to notice the addendum."

By now, Reggie was drumming his fingers on the cashier's desk, a sign Enton recognized as his twin's rapidly dwindling patience.

"Per the addendum," the lawyer continued, "you can't sell the shop until you sell all the books."

Reggie barked a laugh. "You're kidding."

"Nope. From what I understand, there's an inventory tracking system here, very state-of-the-art. It keeps tabs on every book that enters and leaves the building. And every book that has entered, or will enter, this shop must be sold before any title transfer can be made."

"So we'll just include the books when someone buys the property. These stupid hunks of paper aren't our problem."

"No, I don't think you understand. *You* must sell the books. To this shop's customers. The books must find their way to new homes before the property can be put on the market. My firm will ask to see a copy of the inventory tracking spreadsheets, which I'm informed can be easily provided." She made this last comment to Sebastian, who had just strode up carrying a cardboard box.

With an amused smirk on his lips, he agreed it could. Sabrina marched up to stand beside her brother. In her small hands she held a fire-engine red pot from which sprung a lush philodendron.

"This can't be legal," said Reggie. "We'll contest the will."

"Oh, it's very legal," said Sebastian. "The senior partner is a friend of mine. He helped your grandfather write it up, then verified, notarized, and legalized the whole thing. It's very airtight," he added with a twinkling grin.

"You knew about this?" Reggie asked, his hands clenched into white-knuckled fists. "You knew about his will? This," Reggie turned to the lawyer, "is obviously an example of undue influence. My grandfather was coerced."

"I have it on good authority he wasn't," the lawyer said evenly. "My senior partner is very thorough with making sure his clients are making decisions of their own volition."

Reggie said nothing. A vein throbbed in his oversized forehead.

"So I guess we're open today?" Sebastian asked cheerily.

Sabrina turned away from the group and marched the philodendron back up to the break room.

CHAPTER FIVE

Many people, myself among them, feel
better at the mere sight of a book.

—Jane Smiley, Thirteen Ways of Looking at
a Novel

"We're trapped. We're trapped with that pit of
a shop," muttered Reggie. He'd been muttering
these same two phrases since learning of the
clause in the will.

In the days since the horrible news, when not
muttering miserably to himself, Reggie had been
holding numerous phone conversations well out
of Enton's earshot. Whenever the phone would
ring, Reggie would scuttle out of the room to take
the call. Each time he'd returned from these secret
chats, he'd worn an expression that was growing
increasingly strained.

"Well, the good news," Enton said, "is that the
shop's on sound financial footing."

His bulbous forehead wrinkling, Reggie

scowled at his twin. "Not enough of a footing to get us into first class. We've got to get rid of those books and sell off that dump."

"I'd hardly call it a dump." Enton regretted the comment as soon as he made it. His brother could deliver some very scathing looks with only the slightest effort.

To avoid a direct hit of Reggie's ire, Enton returned his focus to the kitchen sink. He wiggled the faucet's spout, delicately shifting it to the only position that would make it stop dripping.

Enton inspected the handle for the cold-water tap. "I think the hardware store's having a plumbing sale this—"

"That's it!" Reggie blurted, startling Enton and causing him to knock his elbow into the faucet. Which began dripping once more. "We'll have a sale." Reggie spread both hands in the air, arcing them as if he were tracing the outline of a banner. "Clearance sale. All stock must go. People love those things."

"Aren't those sales usually just come ons? The store has one, then they're still in business a month later?"

"Yeah, but ours will be legit. You go tell Sebastian, and I'll get an ad going in the paper. Full-page spread. Really grab shoppers' attention."

"Won't that be expensive?"

"It'll be worth it." Reggie stood and mimicked a sommelier pouring a bottle of wine. "More champagne for you, sir?"

Enton grinned despite the drip drip dripping of the tap. First-class seats and maybe money leftover to fix the sink. That would certainly be the life.

* * *

"A sale?" Sebastian said as if the word wasn't in his vocabulary.

Enton, unsure how to respond to the clerk's critical tone, darted his eyes to the framed picture on the wall of him and Reggie in their book fort. Something about it kept snatching his attention, but he couldn't say exactly what. Like seeing a shape out of the corner of your eye and thinking it's a person, a bird, or a monster, only to discover it's just a tree limb swaying in the breeze.

"What kind of sale?" Sebastian prodded.

"Oh, you know, like a spring cleaning sale. Be good to get the shelves cleared for once."

"To what? Make a fresh start with new books?"

"Exactly," Enton said vaguely, since Reggie — who was convinced he could find a loophole that would keep him from having to honor Sebastian's severance package contract — had made it clear he didn't want the clerk to know they still planned to sell "the dump".

"But this is a *used* bookstore. We carry a few new titles, but the whole point is that most of the stock isn't fresh. Does this have to do with your brother wanting to sell the place?"

"Stores have sales all the time. We're a store, so we're having a sale, and that's that. Did you question my grandfather like this?"

"No. But then again, he didn't come up with harebrained ideas." When Enton's only response was to fidget on his feet, Sebastian asked, "So, when will this glorious event take place?"

"This weekend," Enton said, relieved to be faced with a question he could answer. Reggie had figured out all the details of what he'd called their marketing plan. "You'll hand out flyers to the customers who come in this week. We'll also put signs in any shop windows that will allow us to. Then the sale starts Friday, and by Sunday, the shelves will be empty."

"For our spring cleaning?" Sebastian said dubiously as he swept a finger across the cashier's desk that proved not to have a speck of dust on it.

"You are very subordinate."

"Someone's been using their word-of-the-day calendar," Sebastian teased amiably. "Fine, I'll do the hustling for the sale, but it's not going to clear the shelves."

"You can't know that."

"Can't I?"

The bell above the door jangled its tune, and in skipped the dark-haired girl. She'd parked her wagon outside, but in her arms were four books. Enton watched her skip a direct line to the gardening section and begin slipping her books into the few empty spaces on the shelves.

"She can't do that," Enton complained.

"Why not?"

"I just told you. We're trying to clear the stock. We can't do that if she brings stock in."

"She takes books, too," Sebastian said simply. "Sabrina," he called, "no more books. We're supposedly spring cleaning the stock."

The girl had one book left in her hand. With a daring look in her eye, she pushed it onto the shelf. She then marched out of the store, narrowly avoiding barreling into Reggie as he entered.

"What's her problem? She find out we're all out of Addams' Family comics, or something?" he asked.

"She's been adding books to the shelves," Enton said, after pulling his brother away from the cashier's desk so Sebastian couldn't eavesdrop. "Adding more stock."

Reggie pulled out his phone and started dialing.

"You're not calling the cops on her, are you? I mean, we can just ask her—"

"Stan's Security? Yeah, I need some cameras installed at Bookman's Bookshop. Today? Really? That'd be perfect. See you in a bit." Reggie ended the call. "He had a job cancel, so he's got time for us."

* * *

Stan was the kind of man who had the workaday appearance of someone whose closet likely contained nothing but overalls. He advised Reggie where three or four cameras could be put up to monitor the floor of the shop.

"Should help you catch whoever's stealing your books."

"Oh, we haven't had anything stolen," said Enton.

"Prevention," Stan said with approval. "Not enough people think ahead like that."

"No, I mean, our problem is someone *adding* books to our shelves."

Stan raised a shaggy, grey eyebrow. "Ain't a normal problem, but it's your business. Did you also want cameras on the cash register and in the break room?" Reggie said they didn't, and Stan shrugged disapprovingly. "Your choice. Now," with the stub of a pencil, he jotted something on a scrap of paper, "that's my quote."

Enton peered over Reggie's shoulder. Even though the cameras were fairly cheap, the total was staggering. They could buy first-class tickets for three vacations with that amount.

"I'll just take the cameras," Reggie said, handing the scrap back to Stan.

"It's old wiring you got in here," Stan warned. "I don't recommend a self-install unless you got experience with electricals."

"I'm sure you don't. Just the cameras will be fine."

Stan sold Reggie the cameras and tried to offer advice for the installation. Advice Reggie promptly disregarded as he pulled out a ladder and cursed his way through mounting his new security system.

CHAPTER SIX

A place is not really a place without a
bookstore.

—Gabrielle Zevin, The Storied Life of A.J.
Fikry

The morning of the sale's first day saw
customers lined up around the block. Some of this
may have been everyone's love of a good book at
a good discount, but some of it may have also
been Reggie mentioning in the ad that the sale
was for a good cause and that every purchase
would help a deserving person in need.

"Isn't that a bit deceitful?" asked Enton when
he'd opened the newspaper and took in the full-
page spread.

"There's not a single lie in that ad. We *need* to
sell this place. And we are two very deserving
individuals."

Even though Enton had to squirm his way
around a few questions about the charity they

were donating to — a boys' club was the best half-truth he could manage — the sale was going splendidly. As Enton and Sebastian both worked the registers to keep up with the sales, customers continually lined up at the cashier's desk with baskets, and even boxes, full of books. Enton couldn't help but feel a little smug when he rang up three orders to Sebastian's one. If only they were working on commission, he thought.

During a rare lull at the register, Enton scanned the store. There were bare shelves. His heart skipped. This really might work. Reggie was a genius. Deceptive, but a genius, nonetheless.

Reggie strode up to and leaned an elbow on the cashier's desk. The look on his face was like a cat who's just discovered how to order same-day cream delivery from the local dairy.

"What's got you so pleased?" Sebastian asked.

"This inventory system," Reggie replied.

"The one you cursed to every end of the universe when I was demonstrating it to you?"

Because as the lawyer had noted, Bookman's Bookshop was the proud early adopter of a state-of-the-art inventory tracking system which kept a meticulous record of every book that came into and every book that left the shop. The technology for this went far above Enton's head, but he understood the basic concept that every single book added to Bookman's stock was tracked and tallied until a happy customer carried it out the door.

"The very one," Reggie said. "Why can't we just delete the list? Then we dump the books, and we can—"

"Get started on that spring cleaning?" asked Sebastian, a knowing look in his eye. Reggie darted a scowl at Enton, who began to grope for excuses and apologies. For what, he wasn't sure, but clearly he'd screwed up somewhere along the line.

"Calm down," Sebastian said, jumping to Enton's defense.

As Mr Nazzar — who, despite it being early June, wore a sweater with a smiling snowman on it — took his books to Enton to make his purchase, Sebastian continued, "Your brother didn't say a word. I wasn't born yesterday, you know. It's obvious you're shifting stock so you can sell this place. As for your idea with the data, it won't work."

"Why not?"

"First off, the inventory report, as part of the contingency in your grandfather's will, automatically goes to your lawyer at the close of every business day. We're doing a bang-up business with this sale, but she's a smart lady.

She's not going to believe you shifted the entire stock in one day.

"And second, the system simply won't allow it. There's off-site backups, override protections, all the wonders of modern technology to keep your data safe." Sebastian looked past Reggie, his face brightening with a welcoming smile. "Ah, Mrs Kelso, have some treasures for us there?"

A slim woman in a sundress hefted a weighty box of books onto the counter. As if his brother had turned into a cartoon character, Enton saw the dollar signs shining in Reggie's eyes at the prospect of such a large order.

"Sure do. What can I get for these?"

"Did you want to trade, or—?"

"No, no, just store credit is fine. Sadly, I don't have time for any book shopping today."

Sebastian, running a hand along the side of the box and barely glancing at its contents, said, "Does fifteen dollars sound fair?"

"What the hell are you doing?" shouted Reggie.

"Assisting a customer," Sebastian said. "Mrs Kelso has books she no longer needs, so—"

"We're *selling* books, not buying them." Reggie yanked the box toward him and peered in. "There's over two dozen titles in there. How many more have you bought?"

"You mean today, or over my lifetime?"

Reggie's hand clenched the box so tightly the cardboard tore under his grip.

The woman, Mrs Kelso, spoke calmly, as if trying to pacify an angry toddler. "It's part of the store philosophy. Mr Bookman always told us that books change lives. So, when we're done with our novels, we bring them back. Then others' lives have the chance to be changed."

"That's a ridiculous way to run a business. This is a bookstore, not a library!" Reggie bellowed. "We sell books. We don't lend them. And we're having a clearance sale. That does not mean a sale to clear *your* shelves. It means clearing ours so we can fly—"

"Fly the proceeds over to the boys' club," Enton threw out before Reggie got them arrested for fraud.

"Boys' club?" asked another customer who had been waiting to be helped. "I was told it was for a literacy group."

"I was told it was for a cat sanctuary," said someone else.

Enton shook his head. Maybe Reggie wasn't such a genius if he couldn't at least stick to the same story.

"It's for all those," said Reggie with a warm smile. "We — that is, my brother and I — selected from among my grandfather's favorite charities, and they will all get an even portion of the sale's profits. But we won't be able to give them our goal amount if we have to waste time buying up *your* books—" he thumped the now-torn cardboard box "—when we could be selling *our* books. Now, go and enjoy the sale. If you browse all the way to the back of the store, you'll find a fresh batch of donut holes. On your way, fill your baskets with books and remember that every purchase is for a good cause."

A few customers watched Reggie as if he were as suspicious as a telemarketer trying to sell them yet another auto warranty, but others went off in search of sweets and bargains.

Sebastian started to hand Mrs Kelso a receipt for store credit, but Reggie snatched it out of his hand and pushed the box of books back toward the woman.

"Not today, ma'am."

Sebastian sighed heavily, but gave Mrs Kelso a conspiratorial wink. When she left the shop, she carried her box without the slightest effort; and Enton, although he'd only caught a glimpse, swore there was no longer a single book inside it.

CHAPTER SEVEN

Fill your house with stacks of books, in all
the crannies and all the nooks.

—Dr Seuss

"So, how did we do?" Reggie asked greedily on the final evening of the sale as he locked the door then hurried over to the computer. Enton didn't need the machine; he could see for himself that they'd done well. There were still plenty of full or partially full shelves, but there were a few empty ones as well. "Come on, Enton, bring up the numbers."

Enton groaned. He wasn't one for technology, but Sebastian had already handed him the laptop that was networked to the office computer's inventory program.

"No, it's that key," Sebastian said patiently as Enton fumbled his way around the spreadsheet that had automatically updated to the latest tally. "There you go." Sebastian pointed to a row.

"That's what we had at the start of the weekend, and that's what we have now." The clerk gave a puckish grin, but Enton's face drooped. Reggie came around to look at the screen. His brow collapsed into a furrow faster than a bowling ball falling from a skyscraper.

"That's it? We had people lining up at the registers almost every minute of the sale. How could we have gotten rid of so little of this junk?"

"Well, before you called a quits to it, we did have a bit of new stock come in," said Sebastian.

"New stock?" Reggie asked, as if he'd completely forgotten the incident with Mrs Kelso.

"Well, technically old stock. People bringing books back in after reading them."

"Enton, does that thing say how many books this idiot added to the stock we're trying to get rid of?"

Enton kept his head down and tapped the keyboard to bring up the column he thought he needed. "Only about two hundred."

"Okay," Reggie said, the word full of relief. "That's not so bad. We sold eighteen hundred, so we're well—"

"No, sorry," Enton said when Sebastian pointed to the screen. "I meant two thousand."

"We sold two thousand?" Reggie enthused. "Even better."

"No, I didn't have the intake column wide enough. We took in two thousand. Sold eighteen hundred."

"So we literally added more stock than we sold at our clearance sale?"

"It would appear so."

"That's it. You," Reggie stabbed his finger at Sebastian, "out of here. I need to talk to my brother." Without a word, Sebastian collected a satchel from under the cashier's desk and left the shop.

Reggie re-locked the door the moment the bell chimed the clerk's departure. He then turned to his brother, a devilish glint in his eyes. "Where's the electrical box in this dump?"

"Electrical box?" Enton asked.

"Yeah, I saw the papers when I was rooting around Gramps's office. This place is insured and I bet the electricals haven't been fixed up for decades. And look." Enton looked to the ceiling where Reggie was pointing and saw nothing but thick, wooden beams. "No sprinkler system. All we gotta do is cross a wire or two. It's genius."

"It is?" Enton asked, unable to keep the squeak out of his question.

"Sure. A couple bare wires touching and, *whoosh*!" Reggie smacked his palms together. "Place'll burn to the ground, books included. All this paper? All this wood framing? It'll be gone before the fire department's halfway here."

"No, come on, Reggie, that's not—"

Enton wanted to say that burning books felt wrong. Even if he didn't like a book, it just seemed like tempting fate to torch novels, dictionaries, even self-help guides. Well, okay, maybe the self-help guides could go. But he knew this plea wouldn't win over his twin. If he was going to keep Reggie from becoming both a fraudster and an arsonist in the same weekend, he had to come up with a less book-focussed argument against a conflagration.

"What I mean is," he continued, "if this place goes up, well, we share that wall with Petra's Pets, and that wall on the other side with Spielman's Bakery. Sylvester Spielman—" who had brought Enton and Sebastian the flakiest, most buttery croissants the previous afternoon "—lives above his shop. We can't risk the lives of kittens and bakers for this."

"I suppose you're right." Reggie, having just found it, slammed the door of the electrical panel shut. "But there's got to be another way."

"Another liquidation sale?" Reggie looked about to object to his brother's suggestion, but Enton barreled on. "Not like this one. We can make things ten cents a book. We'll shift stock like an avalanche."

"And we're not taking in any new stock. That's going to be on a big sign out front. I'll get another ad posted tomorrow."

Enton just hoped it wasn't a full-page one. He wasn't sure their credit limit could handle it.

Chapter Eight

A book is a version of the world. If you do not like it, ignore it; or offer your own version in return.

—Salman Rushdie

"*Another* spring cleaning sale?" Sebastian asked the following Tuesday when Enton told him of Reggie's latest scheme. "Wasn't that the point of last weekend's little event?"

"That was just a practice run. This one's the real deal, and stuff's going to be flying off the shelves. I mean, who wouldn't pay a dime for a book?" Enton turned from his chore of taping up a sign stating '*No books being bought*' to the window. He'd already placed a similarly worded placard by the cash register. "Or do you think we should make it a nickel? Five-cent fiction, nickel non-fiction. Has a nice ring to it, don't you think?"

"You do have a way with words," Sebastian said, then greeted his customer, Rafi Nazzar, who had just placed three books on the cashier's desk. He was currently dressed in his Sikh turban and a sweater featuring Rudolph, whose red nose blinked on and off in a steady rhythm. "Nice sweater, Mr Nazzar."

"Another of Mr Bookman's," he said, tugging gently at the gaudy garment to show it off. "There's twenty-six more. Can you imagine? I will be the talk of the town."

"You certainly will," said Sebastian with a warm, indulgent smile. "That'll be thirty cents."

Sebastian dropped three dimes into the till, and Mr Nazzar bid the two men farewell, telling them he'd be back the next day to show off another of the "fine pieces of fashion art" Mr Bookman had left him.

If three dimes seems inexpensive for three books, it is. But Reggie had decided not to wait for the weekend to start his sale. After all, why should they pass up a full week of getting the shelves emptied of all that unwanted stock and launching themselves closer to the first-class lounge?

"I just don't think this is the weekend for it," said Sebastian.

"Why not?" Enton asked. "It's the neighborhood's spring festival, isn't it? Parade, face painting, and all that other stuff going on?

People'll be flocking to this very street. We'll be swamped."

Sebastian made a noncommittal noise of skeptical agreement. From outside, Sabrina waved at him, then furrowed her brow at the sign Enton had just posted. Once again, she had her wagon in tow.

"Why's she always dragging that wagon around?" asked Enton.

"She carries things for people. Gets a quarter a load. She's very enterprising."

"Your parents don't worry about her roaming the streets all day?"

"We've always been very independent."

Another customer, a balding man with a dark ring of remaining hair circling his scalp, placed his purchases on the counter.

As Sebastian chatted and rang up the order, Enton's gaze drifted to the photo of him and Reggie in their fort. He kept meaning to take a closer look at the picture, but the store was always so busy, and Reggie was constantly on him about pushing stock and doing whatever it took to convince people to buy more, more, more.

Reggie had even suggested that Enton drop extra books into people's baskets without their noticing.

Although the ethics of doing so nagged at him,

Enton did manage this bit of retail trickery a couple times. But since those two times, each of his attempts ended in failure. And sometimes embarrassment.

Because since those two moments of success, whenever Enton tried to surreptitiously slip a book into an unguarded basket, something would happen. Sebastian would let out a chortling laugh, Sabrina and a herd of kids over at the children's section would send up a delighted squeal, Sebastian would make an announcement on the P.A. system (Enton wasn't even aware they had a P.A. system), or some other distraction would cause the unsuspecting shopper to turn. The basket not being where he'd aimed, Enton would end up dropping the book on the floor. Customers were beginning to think he was very clumsy.

"And thank you, Mr Gordon," Sebastian said, handing the man a hefty sack of books.

"Fine weekend for a book sale," said Mr Gordon. "You guys going to set up some tables out front? Weather should be excellent for a sidewalk sale."

Enton thought this was a great idea. And who knows? With all those books out in the open, completely unattended, any shoplifters would have an easy time of it. It wasn't exactly *selling* books, but it was a way to whittle down that pesky inventory tally.

"A good idea, Mr Gordon," said Sebastian, "but not this weekend, I'm afraid. It's going to be far too nasty out."

Both Mr Gordon and Enton glanced out the window to see a bright blue sky. Mr Gordon nodded sagely. "Suppose you're right. You always are. I don't know how you do it."

"If only I could pick lottery numbers," smiled Sebastian, as if this were the expected thing to say in a familiar conversation.

"Right you are. I'd wish you luck with the sale, but since I don't want to see this place go, it would only be a false wish."

"Nasty?" Enton said as soon as the man was out the door. "My weather report," Enton held up his phone, "says it's supposed to be sunny with highs in the mid-seventies."

"You can't rely on those things. They're notoriously inaccurate. It's going to be howling. I know you won't listen to me, but I'd consider putting off the sale until next weekend. There's no point in Reggie wasting money on ads when no one's going to be shopping."

Enton tried to act casual as he strode away from the cashier's desk, but curiosity got the better of him and he raced up to the office. He had to get on the computer and check every weather report he could find.

But when he flung open the office door, Reggie was inside. With a woman.

Sorry. Not like that.

Reggie was on one side of the desk, the woman was on the other, and everyone's clothes were zipped and buttoned. Still, Enton was surprised by her presence. Namely, because, in her crisply tailored business attire, she looked very official, very much like someone he should be meeting with as well. Enton stood there a moment, trying to catch his breath.

"Thank you for your time, Mr Bookman. I'll be in touch."

The woman stood, then Reggie stood, and Enton suddenly felt as if he should stand even more than he already was. Briefcase in hand, she brushed past Enton, giving him little more than a tilt of her pointed chin as she left.

"What was that about?" Enton asked sharply the moment the woman was down the stairs.

"She's a developer. She wants to buy the place," Reggie said, a gleam in his eyes.

"When did this happen?"

"You've seen me on the phone. I've been negotiating. She just came by so I could sign the papers."

"Without consulting me? Without getting the lawyer's approval?"

"Didn't have time. You gotta act fast with these real estate deals. And this one's not only fast, it's more than we could have hoped for. As long as the place remains in the same condition, we'll finalize the deal in a couple weeks."

"The books too?" Enton asked, not entirely understanding the flicker of dismay in his gut.

Reggie's face darkened. "No. Unfortunately, they're not interested in the books, which is why we still gotta find a way around that stupid contingency in Gramps's will before the deal can go through."

"But what's she want this place for?"

"Not the place, the block. She says this shop has always been the lynchpin. Says as soon as we sell, the others will too."

"But why?"

Reggie pushed a brochure across the desk. On the front was a modern building, all glass and steel and other materials that Enton supposed were meant to look classy, but to him looked cold and cheap. The text read, *'Spare ALL expense on your next investment home.'*

Enton looked up from the brochure. Reggie answered the question on his face. "They buy up blocks in trendy areas. Convert the existing buildings into apartments. Modernize them a bit. Do something with the interiors — I don't know what exactly — and jazz up the exteriors using the cheapest construction possible. Then they advertise the units on high-end real estate websites and charge rich people thousands a month for rent. It's genius, really," he added admiringly.

"And you're really considering this?" asked Enton, who'd always admired the solid construction of the shop, its decorative façade, and the stylish row of connected buildings that were still in perfect shape despite, or perhaps because of, being over a hundred years old.

"Not considering. It's done. Assuming we get rid of the stock, of course. These books have gotta be gone by the end of the month, or..." Reggie shifted uncomfortably.

"Or what?"

"Or we'll be in breach of contract and I'll have to pay a percentage of the agreed-upon sale price."

Enton darted a look at the wall calendar. "Christ, Reg, the end of the month's barely two weeks away. We can't afford—"

"Stop fretting. It's no big deal. It's a small percentage, and more than likely, it's just some crap their legal team says they have to throw in.

Besides, we're already making a good dent in the stock. After the sale this weekend, the shelves will be so empty there'll be an echo in here. And whatever books we have left on Sunday, we offer for a penny. You'll see, people can't resist a discount like that. That damn inventory sheet will be blank in no time."

"Sebastian says we'll have bad weather. Do you think we ought to move the sale to next weekend?" Enton glanced at the calendar. "We'd still have time before the deal goes through."

Or falls through, he couldn't help but think.

"Can't do it. I already paid for a full-page ad in the papers."

"Papers?" Enton asked, emphasizing the plural. Reggie was only supposed to place a single ad in the neighborhood circular, and even that had been out of their budget.

"Sure, they're all managed by the same editor. Figured that made things easy, so why not? We've got to attract customers. It's more than worth the cost. No, not cost. Investment."

"And how much did we *invest*?"

"Not important. We'll pay it back when we sell the place."

"But where did you get the money?"

"Simple. I paid with my credit card. Won't have to pay for at least a month, and we get loads of airline miles. Miles that could be used for upgrades," Reggie added, like someone dangling a strip of bacon in front of a basset hound.

"Upgrades?"

"VIP lounge."

Enton grinned, imagining rubbing elbows with the famous people he assumed passed their leisure time in airport VIP lounges.

CHAPTER NINE

Rainy days should be spent at home with a cup of tea and a good book.

—Bill Patterson

The Thursday before this second sale saw calm weather, sunny skies, and still no hint of trouble from the four radar images Enton had been keeping his eye on all week. He went to sleep that night with his bedroom window open to enjoy the night air and the light of a bright full moon shining above.

At three a.m., thick clouds obscured the moon. The room went dark, but Enton slept on.

At four a.m., Enton stirred and, still half-asleep, pulled a quilt over himself to fend off the chilly air flooding into the room.

At five a.m., Enton found himself in a dream of sailing on the yacht of a celebrity he'd met in the VIP lounge. Enton stood on the bow of the yacht, and in his sleep he muttered, "I'm the king of the world." He jerked awake just as a massive wave rose up before him.

Enton touched his fingers to his face. It was damp. Not just damp, but wet. Slowly coming to his senses, he realized water was lashing in from the open window. He jumped up, slammed the sash down, swayed a moment from getting up too quickly, then stared outside, hardly believing what he was seeing.

It was indeed howling. Enton had never been in a hurricane or a tropical storm, but those were the first words that came to mind as he watched the neighbors' fir trees whipping in the wind, the rain falling sideways, and a garbage bin go thumping down the street in the gale.

But the four radar systems he'd been tracking? And his deep dive into the weather lore of the Pacific Northwest? Not to mention the six weather reports he'd watched before going to bed. None of these had indicated a storm was on its way. Surely meteorologists couldn't be *this* bad at their jobs.

So how had Sebastian known? For a brief moment, Enton wondered if Sebastian had caused the storm. Which Enton decided was solid proof he needed a first-class vacation.

He told himself he was an idiot and went to start the coffee as a message came through his phone announcing the neighborhood spring festival had been cancelled on account of the weather.

* * *

Driving to the shop was a slow and strange ordeal. The streets around the block where Bookman's Bookshop stood were flooded in water up to the curb, whereas getting down the street on which Enton's and Reggie's house stood had merely involved driving through deep puddles.

Hardly anyone was out. Who could blame them? A few grim-faced drivers inched through the stream of rainwater rippling past the bookstore, but no one was out walking, browsing, or visiting the shops. Although Enton did catch sight of a gleeful man paddling by on an inflatable raft.

"Why is it just this block?" asked Enton, even though a tiny voice was telling him the answer: Sebastian had something to do with it. After all, the clerk had known about the rain when no one else had.

"Probably because this area's closer to the river. You know how these old storm drains are always getting clogged up. I bet if we go all the way to the Esplanade—" a pedestrian path along the Willamette River "—we'd be up to our butts in water."

Reggie was probably right. It made sense. Their home was farther away from the river than the shop, and their street hadn't been flooded. Sebastian indeed. Enton chuckled to himself.

"Do you think this is funny?"

"No, it's a mess."

"It's not just a mess. It's going to ruin our sale. Who's going to come out in this?"

Enton considered mentioning the guy in the inflatable raft, but thought better of it. Thankfully, by the time Reggie pulled the wrong way into a parking spot, the rain had eased off to little more than a steady trickle of fat drops. Still, to avoid stepping into calf-deep water, Enton had to maneuver over the gear stick and exit through the driver's side door that let out onto the curb.

As Reggie slipped a key into the shop door's lock, Sebastian sauntered up to them wearing a bright yellow rain jacket with rubber galoshes to match.

"People will certainly be looking for something to cozy up with today, that's for sure," the clerk said, his voice as bright as his rain gear. Reggie grunted and wrenched on the doorknob, his set of keys jangling in the lock. Reggie then cursed, stepped back, and drove his shoulder into the door.

"Is the lock stuck?" Enton asked.

"No, the damn lock isn't stuck. But the door is," Reggie said and gave the door another bash with his shoulder. The window pane rattled, but the door didn't budge.

"Oh, it'll be swollen from the damp," said Sebastian.

"Swollen from the damp?" Reggie snapped. "This is Portland. It's damp eight months out of the year, and I know damn well the shop didn't close down every time there was a little rain."

Enton and Sebastian both looked from Reggie to the water flowing down the street, then back to Reggie with looks that said, "A little rain?"

"No, of course not," said Sebastian. "Didn't your grandfather tell you? After a dry spell, the door can withstand wet weather as long as you give it a quick coat of oil when rain is expected. This," he gestured to the cloudy sky, "is not expected. The door must have sucked up the moisture better than a paper towel in a TV ad. Strange, isn't it?"

"It's not strange. It's just physics," Reggie grumbled and made to ram the door again.

"I wouldn't do that," advised Sebastian. "Believe me, bigger men than you have tried to overcome that door. A few now have permanent shoulder issues."

"But we've got the sale," Reggie complained. "How long until this thing dries out?"

"Usually a couple days. Once the rain stops," Sebastian said, leaning out from the awning to glance ruefully up at the sky. Enton peered out from under the awning as well. It was still drizzling, but the worst of the rain had let up, and he thought he could make out a blue patch amongst the steely grey.

"But I've run ads." Reggie's face went pale. "Do you know how much I've invested in those ads?"

"You could try next weekend," Sebastian suggested. "I think you'll have to because this weekend is a wash. Even the festival has been cancelled. Look, how about I come by every few hours to see if the door's come unstuck, and I'll call you if there's any change. You," Sebastian looked Reggie up and down, "you don't look well. You should probably get home and under some warm blankets."

"A drink," Reggie muttered through chattering teeth. "I need a drink."

"But it's only nine a.m.," said Enton.

"You're right. No bars are going to be open yet. Enton, drive me home. I hear a bottle of Glenfiddich calling my name."

CHAPTER TEN

Books are a uniquely portable magic.

—Stephen King, On Writing

Reggie had finished half of the bottle of whisky when he announced he'd just had the brilliant idea to move the sale to the following weekend. Enton then winced as Reggie called up the newspapers to complain, in scotch-slurred words, that the ads had been printed incorrectly, that the newspaper had gotten the date wrong, and that they owed him a re-printing of the ads, free of charge.

The idea, although Enton thought it would be a reasonable request in any other circumstance, didn't work. The editor got on the phone and told Reggie he had the proofs on which Reggie had signed and dated his approval, that they wouldn't re-run the ads for free, and — after Reggie tried a different tack — that, no, Reggie could not have his money back just because the rain had spoiled his sale.

"Are we still having the sale next weekend?" asked Enton. "Even without the ads?"

"Yes, we are," replied Reggie as he emphatically tossed back another shot. "I'm putting in an order to the printer right now. We'll get some signs made and put them up all around town. Far and wide. Far and wide," Reggie said as he swayed drunkenly in his chair. "We're selling those damn books, come hell or high water. Okay, well, maybe not high water, but those shelves are going to be empty by closing time next Sunday."

* * *

Unsurprisingly, Enton was given the chore of collecting the signs from the printer. When the shopkeeper handed him Reggie's credit card receipt, the off-brand cereal in Enton's gut solidified into a spiky ball.

With what Reggie already owed the newspaper, these signs surely had to be pushing them close to a financial cliff. Could debt collectors seize the house over a few unpaid ads? Enton didn't know, but worried about the billable hours if he called the lawyer to ask.

The store. They just needed to sell the store

and it'd all be fine.

Motivated, if not enthused, Enton trudged through the drizzle and nailed up newly printed signs on utility poles and notice boards across much of Southeast Portland.

* * *

In the week leading up to the sale, Enton worked at the shop and felt both a wave of relief and dismay as he watched a few shelves go bare.

On the day before the sale's official start, while working the register with Sebastian, Enton again noticed a tattered book transform into something nearly new when the clerk handed it back to a customer after ringing it up.

"How do you do that?" asked Enton as the till chimed.

"This button here," Sebastian replied and pressed a key that opened the cash drawer. The chime sounded again when he pushed it closed.

"No, the thing with the books. They change from beat-up to brand-new in your hands. I've seen it more than once."

"Perhaps it's time for an eye exam?" Sebastian said as he rang up the six books a pink-haired man had just brought up.

"Don't think so. Had perfect vision all my life."

"What can I say? Perhaps when a book finds the right reader, it blooms into its full potential."

"That's poetry, man," said the customer, handing Sebastian six dimes for the books he was now examining more closely. "Books change people. So, you know, why shouldn't people change books?"

"Every story takes its reader on a slightly different journey," said Sebastian.

"Yeah, man. Books are magic." The customer pointed a bony finger toward the sign over the door. "That right there, that's poetry too."

"Actually, it's a misquote of Stephen King," Enton said. The man looked at him like a child who's just been told the Easter Bunny doesn't exist. Enton couldn't help but apologize.

"This place really closing down?" the customer asked as Reggie marched up to the cashier's desk.

Enton glanced at his watch. Yep, two hours had passed. Like clockwork, Reggie had been coming down from the office every two hours and reporting to Enton the latest inventory count.

"It is," Reggie boasted, then smacked the stack of poetry books the man had just bought. "So, if you want any more inspiration, or whatever these are, you best get it now. In fact, why not buy all of them?"

"All of what?" the man asked, clearly confused.

"The whole poetry section. It's yours for five bucks."

"You messing with me?"

"Nope. Five bucks and all the iambic pentameter you could ever want is yours."

The man dug in his pocket, examined what he'd pulled out, and grinned when he saw a crumpled five-dollar bill amongst the debris.

"Enton, get this gentleman a box and help him out with his wise purchase."

Once Enton had cleared most of the poetry section — not all, since the man refused to take Shakespeare's sonnets, calling them too bourgeois — and sent a very happy customer on his way, Reggie leaned back on the cashier's desk looking proud of himself.

"That's how you do it. None of this one-book-here-one-book-there BS. Volume, boys. Sell in volume every chance you get. Hell, sell the posters off the walls while you're at it."

"I take it the inventory count is going well?" Sebastian asked critically.

"Sure is. You might want to polish off your resume, because Bookman's stock is disappearing faster than wallets at a pickpocket convention."

CHAPTER ELEVEN

Reading is important. If you know how to read, then the whole world opens up to you.

- Barack Obama

The weekend of the sale arrived. Friday was no busier than usual, but Enton wrote that off to it still being a workday. People didn't have time to shop, and once they were off work, they wanted to go out, not browse for books.

But when only a few customers, regulars who Enton now knew by name, trickled in on Saturday, Reggie took notice.

"Did you put up the signs?" he asked, the question full of accusation.

"Of course I did. All over the place. There's probably not a utility pole within a three-mile radius without one."

"I'm going to go look. And I swear if I find even one naked pole—"

The eyes of a stout, elderly woman holding a photo book about Poland went wide and she clutched the book to her chest.

"Mrs Gursky, can I help you with that?" offered Sebastian.

The woman scooted away from Reggie and over to the clerk. When she told him the book had pictures of the village she grew up in, it was with a slight eastern European accent.

"I didn't mean *Pole* as in the people, ma'am," said Reggie. "I meant *pole*. You know, as in dancer."

This did nothing to appease the woman, but Reggie had no time to bother with tending to upset customers. He needed to verify how much of an idiot his brother really was.

"Enton, in the car. Now!" Reggie demanded, then stormed out. After giving Mrs Gursky an apologetic shrug of his shoulders, Enton followed after his twin.

Reggie, gripping the wheel like it had done something to truly offend him, drove with the determination of a man who had a point to prove. Although Enton tried to make small talk, Reggie wordlessly steered the car up and down block after block, glowering at every utility pole he passed.

And Enton understood why.

Not a single post bore a sign announcing the sale. There were plenty of signs about literacy being power and the worlds you could discover in books, but not one scrap of a flyer about the marvelous discounts to be had at Bookman's Bookshop.

Finally, after twenty long minutes of chowder-thick silence, Reggie veered the car back in the direction of the shop. "You told me you put up the signs," he stated flatly.

"I did."

"So where are they?"

"How should I know? What?" Enton squawked in response to his brother's fiery stare. "Do you think I got up early this morning and took them all down?"

"I think maybe you never put them up in the first place. I see how you and Sebastian get along. I see you with your customer service. Do you think helping some old woman find just the right book about cats is going to get you first-class tickets? Do you think ringing up orders with a friendly smile is going to set us up for life? We're selling the shop, whether you want to or not."

"Whether I want to or not? What's that mean?"

"I mean," said Reggie as he maneuvered the car along the narrow streets, "that you no longer seem very interested in selling this dump."

"Of course I want to sell it. You're being an idiot," Enton said with less conviction than he expected. In his mind flashed an image of the framed photo on the wall near the register.

He and Reggie used to love Gramps's store. Of course, they had also loved wandering next door to Spielman's Bakery for samples of fresh bread slathered in butter. Or to Petra's Pets, the other neighboring shop, to play with the kittens and chat with the resident parrot. But what they had especially enjoyed was simply being at Bookman's Bookshop. They'd spent summer days amongst the stacks, reading books, dusting shelves, unpacking boxes, and they had loved every minute of it.

And then there was Gramps himself. He had never seemed to work too hard, he'd never had to put in long hours, but yet he was always flush with cash. Not ostentatiously wealthy, but he was always happy and always able to take them on a yearly vacation of their choice — then on the vacations of his choice once they moved out. His home was always in good repair, his clothes were always crisp and looking like new, and he never missed a chance to eat at a nice restaurant. Was that all due to the shop? A good life, an easy life, a satisfying life without financial want?

A first-class trip of a lifetime would be nice,

Enton thought, but then what? They'd still come back to a broken-down house, broken-down car, and broken-down senses of contentment.

"Enton!" snapped Reggie. "You getting out, or are you going to daydream all day?"

Enton looked out the car window to see they were at the bookshop. Through the window, Sebastian was helping a woman who smiled with delight at her finds. And her smile made Enton smile. Smile, that is, until Reggie slammed the car door shut and marched toward the shop's entrance, complaining about the lack of customers.

Chapter Twelve

A room without books is like a body
without a soul.

—Cicero

No sales records were at risk of toppling that Saturday. And Sunday was no better. In fact, the shop had been strangely quiet for a Sunday. When Enton brought this up to Sebastian, the clerk merely shrugged and said it was probably because the neighborhood council had suddenly opted to call off that week's Sunday market. The market that never failed to attract people who, once finished purchasing their organic vegetables and artisan bread, were more than eager to browse the neighborhood's shops, make impulse purchases, and show little concern when they returned home with empty wallets.

At five p.m. that Sunday, Reggie locked the shop's door and turned the sign to closed.

"That's it. New plan."

"This should be interesting," quipped Sebastian. "Are we going to throw books at drivers from the highway overpass?"

"Not a bad idea, but I was thinking something less potentially deadly. Now, box up everything we have left."

"We're throwing entire boxes of books at drivers?" asked Enton. Sebastian's chuckle brought a scowl to Reggie's face.

"No, we're donating the rest of the stock to charity. Box up what's left and keep track of the inventory so we can update the spreadsheet. Every book must go? Well, they're going to go."

"But aren't you supposed to *sell* the books?" asked Sebastian.

"Technically, the books will be sold. By the charity shop. Same difference, right? Go on," Reggie clapped his hands twice in quick succession, "get packing. And don't forget to track the inventory. I don't want to have to hunt down some damn chick-lit novel you've left behind."

As Reggie slipped out of the shop, telling his brother he had to run an errand, Enton began filling boxes with books. He finished the travel section, the craft section, and the history section. But when he got to the poetry section, he stopped, unable to believe his eyes.

There, on the very shelf whose entire contents

(except for the bourgeois sonnets) he himself had boxed up for the pink-haired customer only days before, was a full array of poetry books. Dickinson, Auden, Frost, all hanging out together once again.

Had Sebastian taken in new stock? Or had the books somehow replenished themselves? Enton shook his head. What an idiotic thought. And what did it matter? Because for Frost, Auden, Dickinson, and all the rest, it was time to pack up for a trip to the Sunny Second Chances Charity Shop.

Enton's back and arms were aching by the time Reggie strode back into the shop, twirling a set of keys on his index finger as he whistled a carefree tune.

"Where've you been?" Enton asked.

"Well, we're not going to haul all these boxes in the Civic, are we?" Reggie gestured out the window.

Parked in front of Bookman's, as out of place on the narrow street as an elephant in an antique store, was a moving truck from a rental company Enton had never heard of. Dirt cascaded off the loading door as Reggie forced it open; and once opened, Enton swore he saw something scurry away from the light streaming in.

After loading the back with box after box of

books, Reggie drove the van home. In their car, Enton followed the truck's trail of smoky exhaust.

"Tell me again, why didn't we just leave the truck at the bookshop?" Enton asked that evening as he took a bite of frozen pizza. And yes, it was still somewhat frozen due to the element in the Bookman brothers' oven giving out five minutes after Reggie had put the pizza in.

"Because the contents of that truck are vital to our future as first-class travelers. I'm not letting it out of my sight." Reggie then folded his slice of pizza in half and held it between his hands, trying to warm it.

Chapter Thirteen

I have always imagined paradise will be a
kind of library.

—Jorge Luis Borges

The next morning, Enton woke with aching
shoulders and a head still full of disturbing
dreams in which boxes of books suddenly split
open, erupted like volcanoes, and spewed their
contents back onto the store's shelves.

In the kitchen, Reggie had already settled in to
a breakfast of leftover pizza and chocolate milk.
Enton groggily poured a cup of coffee. Then, with
his shoulders protesting, he tugged and pulled
and grunted to get the wonky cabinet door open
to grab a box of cereal. When he took a seat at the
table, Reggie was smiling as gleefully as someone
who's just watched twenty minutes of cat videos.

"What's got you so chipper?"

"Today's the day we get rid of the books. Just
in time for the deal to go through Wednesday."

"Wednesday?" Still groggy from sleep, Enton only just recalled it was indeed Monday. "I thought the developers were giving us until the end of the month to get rid of the books."

"They were, but I figured why wait? This donation idea of mine takes care of the biggest obstacle, so I called them this morning while you were still snoring, and I moved things up. Why delay our future as millionaires, am I right?"

"But if we don't get the books taken care of, the deal falls through and you owe them for breach of contract. How much was that, again?" Enton asked, even though he was sure Reggie hadn't told him what the exact fee would be. Which had to mean it was substantial. "Or did you also change that part of the contract without talking to me first?"

"Calm down. I've got it sorted. Should've done this when we first learned about that stupid clause in Gramps's will."

Enton spooned dry cereal into his mouth and drank his coffee, both of which dropped like stones into his gut. As soon as he'd finished, Enton got dressed, with Reggie shouting at him to get a move on. By the time Enton came down from his bedroom, his twin was already behind the wheel of the rental truck. Enton climbed into the passenger seat and as soon as he closed the door, Reggie turned the key in the ignition.

The van's engine made a sound like a mechanical cat whose tail has just been smashed in a door. Reggie released the key, then tried again. The mechanical cat now sounded as if it were undergoing a neuter surgery without the benefit of anesthesia. Reggie cursed, punched the dashboard, then turned the key again.

This time, thankfully, the mechanical cat had gone off to chase the great animatronic mouse in the sky. Reggie filled the silence with more cursing that was now drawing the neighbors' notice. Reggie dug out his phone and pounded his finger against the screen.

"Who are you calling?"

"The company who rented me this waste of metal."

Although pressed firmly against Reggie's ear, Enton heard the call ring six times. Reggie pulled the phone away, hung up, and stabbed out the number again. More ringing until Enton heard a robotic female voice telling his brother the office was currently closed and to please call back during normal business hours. It then failed to mention when those business hours might be.

"Those bastards. Those unbelievable bastards. How are we supposed to get the books to the charity shop if this pile of bolts won't go?" As he shouted each of these sentences, Reggie pounded his palms against the steering wheel.

"Doesn't that charity shop do pick ups?" Enton asked, recalling seeing the brightly painted trucks driving around town.

"What are you talking about? We're not donating a pick-up. We're donating books."

"No, not a pick-up truck. A pick up, as in one of their drivers comes by to collect your donation. I think you can schedule one if you have items you can't bring in yourself."

"And you didn't think of mentioning this before I laid out money for this hunk of junk?"

"Mention it? And when would I have done that?" Enton snapped, his heart pounding in his ears. "You'd already rented this thing, made the arrangements with the developers, and all the rest of this without asking me once for my opinion."

"Opinion? *You* have an opinion? It's money, Enton. You don't have an opinion about money. You just want more of it. Everyone wants more of it, and I've been doing exactly what it takes to get us more of it."

"I'm not sure if it's worth it," Enton said, surprising himself.

"Not worth it? Millions of dollars? VIP lounge? Free-flowing champagne? That's not worth selling some shop that doesn't mean anything to anyone?"

"It seems to mean something to plenty of people."

"Are those other people going to give us millions of dollars? No. If people want books, there's a library six blocks away." Reggie went quiet, and Enton didn't like the sneaky grin that crawled across his twin's lips. "Tell you what, if that stupid shop means so much to you, I'll sell you my share. You can twiddle away your life with old ladies and their romance novels while I enjoy the easy life."

"You'd really do that?" Enton asked, picturing the possibility ahead of him. He had no idea how he'd get the money, but managing the bookshop didn't sound that far-fetched. Maybe he could start a crowdfunding campaign. The news was always going on about how those things racked up scads of money in only a few weeks. It would be perfect if—

"What's that kid doing here?" Reggie asked, snapping Enton out of his daydream of community camaraderie.

Strolling down the sidewalk with her wagon rattling behind was Sabrina. "That is one weird kid. Ah well, at least she's getting her exercise. So, what do you say, Enton? Think you can come up with a few million by Wednesday?"

"Wednesday?"

"Yeah, the agreement with the developer," Reggie said smugly. "It's not just going to disappear because you've got a thing for books all the sudden. I'd have to pull out of it to sell you my share, and that means we'd have to pay them for breach of contract."

"Right," muttered Enton, reality slapping him in the face with a concrete glove. What was he thinking, anyway? A bookshop owner? Him? He wanted to travel. He wanted the VIP lounge. He wanted the big stretch-out seats on the plane. Didn't he?

Enton gestured to the phone in Reggie's hand. "You gonna call the charity shop to do the pick up, or what?"

Grinning the entire time, Reggie dialed the number and spoke to the operator. The charity didn't normally do same-day collections, but as they already had a truck in the area, she agreed the driver could come by within a couple hours.

"Must be our lucky day. Just think of it. Us. Millionaires," Reggie said dreamily as he hooked his arm over Enton's throbbing shoulders.

CHAPTER FOURTEEN

I guess there are never enough books.

—John Steinbeck

Soon after the Sunny Second Chances Charity man showed up, Reggie and Enton began shifting boxes out of their broken down rental and into the back of the brightly painted collection truck. Reggie was just handing up the final box when Enton saw a flash of sunlight reflecting off glass.

"Whoa, hold on. Not that." He jogged over and took the framed photo from the box. "How did that get in there?"

"Don't know. I didn't pack it," said Reggie, peering over Enton's shoulder at the picture. "We were cute little shits, weren't we?"

"That it?" droned the collection man. "I got a schedule to keep."

Reggie checked their rental truck one final time. The back was empty. Every book gone. The deal would go through. They would be rich. It was enough to make him ignore the guy's rude tone.

"It certainly is," he said cheerily. "By the way, you wouldn't happen to have a spare dime?"

"A dime?" the man asked, as if he'd never heard of such a thing.

"Yeah, a dime," Reggie responded, his voice sweet and bordering on obsequious. "Ten cents. I wouldn't normally ask, but..."

Eying Reggie like he'd lost enough marbles to fill a swimming pool, the man dug into his pocket and pulled out a quarter. "There, knock yourself out."

"You don't know what this means to me." Reggie held the coin between his thumb and forefinger, smiling idiotically at the silver treasure. Then, without a hint of sarcasm, he added, "And thanks so much for your friendly service."

"Yeah, whatever." The guy slapped a donation receipt into Reggie's palm, hauled the rear metal door down with a clatter and bang, then drove off without saying goodbye.

"You know what they say, Enton?"

"What's that, Reggie?"

"When one door closes, another one opens."

"The door to the VIP lounge?"

"Exactly," Reggie said with a good-natured chuckle.

"What was that asking him for change all about?" Enton knew his brother had racked up some hefty expenses lately, but he didn't think begging for dimes was the speediest way to settle the bills.

"He took our books and gave me money. So, technically, we sold him those books. That lawyer can't complain one bit."

Reggie then pulled out his phone and began tapping out a number.

"Who are you calling now?" asked Enton.

"The lawyer," Reggie said, as if that shouldn't be obvious. "She's gotta verify the stock's been sold before— Yes, hello, Reggie Bookman here. I am indeed. No, I don't really need to speak with her, but if you could tell her to come by Bookman's Bookshop as soon as possible— I realize she's a busy woman, but my brother and I are very important people." Reggie grinned with self-importance. "So if you could just tell her to pop by, I'm sure she'd love nabbing some billable hours while getting out and about." Reggie hung up the phone. "We better get to the shop. She'll probably be there any minute now."

In fact, "any" minute turned into exactly one hundred and twenty-four minutes when the lawyer cut short her lunch hour to stop by her clients' shop. Sebastian walked her up to the office, then pulled up the inventory records on the computer.

The lawyer, as if she could work both eyes independently, scanned the shop's computer records and her own physical records at the same time, running a finger along the ledger Sebastian assured her was up-to-date. After forty-seven minutes of scrutiny and triple checking, she closed the ledger and addressed the twins, who were sitting expectantly across the desk from her.

"You've got a buyer lined up already?" she asked.

"Yep, deal goes through on Wednesday," replied Reggie.

"And you've informed them of the contingency?"

"Contingency? Oh, the books being sold. I may have glossed over that one. The problem's been settled, so there's really no need to bother them with the details, right?"

"The problem is not settled," the lawyer said flatly, and from the corner of his eye, Enton swore he saw Sebastian's lips flick the briefest of smiles.

"Not settled? We shifted the stock," Reggie said, his voice pitching high with defiant disbelief. "The shelves are empty. Those records are obviously mistaken."

"They're not," Sebastian said without a hint of doubt.

"According to the ledger," said the lawyer before Reggie verbally erupted, "there are still two books unaccounted for."

"Two books. You're really going to nitpick over two books?"

"It's a requirement of the will. All the books must be sold."

"But they could've been shoplifted. They could've gone moldy and been thrown out. They could've—" Reggie's eyes went wide and he stabbed a finger at Sebastian. "That sister of yours. She stole them off the truck. We saw her in front of our house this morning. You sent her to ruin us just so you could keep your job."

"That is a very elaborate theory," Sebastian said evenly. "Have you considered writing fiction yourself? An imagination like that shouldn't go to waste."

Reggie lunged for Sebastian. And he might have succeeded in the attack if he had bothered to remember there was another human and a sturdy wooden chair between them.

As his brother barreled past him, Enton reached out to grab him by the waist, but it was too late. Reggie had already tripped over the chair leg and was in the process of falling to the floor, face first. Enton, his arms around Reggie's waist, landed on top of his twin, looking for all the world like an unflinching rugby player whose teammates will declare MVP by the end of the match for such a game-saving move.

Sebastian, for his part, remained where he'd been standing. His only concession to the thwarted attack was to arch an eyebrow as he observed the pile of Bookmans.

"I assume you're done?" the lawyer stated as Enton stumbled his way upright then held out a hand to help Reggie off the floor.

Reggie plopped down in his seat and glared sulkily at the lawyer.

"Good," she said. "Now, you have the rest of the day and tomorrow. According to the tracking system, as Sebastian has explained it to me, the books have to be in this shop somewhere. They're bound to turn up. If you want the deal to go through, simply look around."

The lawyer then glanced at her watch and made a note of the billable hours.

Chapter Fifteen

If you don't like to read, you haven't found the right book.

— J.K. Rowling

The instant the lawyer was out the door, Reggie, like a general determined to find a missing soldier, ordered a search for the books. Sebastian started to follow Enton, but Reggie blocked his path. "Not you."

"I'm quite good at finding things."

"I don't trust you. You're up to something. I don't know what it is, but, well, I know it's something."

"The only thing I'm up to is going for a stroll and then picking up some lunch. Want me to bring back anything?"

"Those two books."

Sebastian pointed to the scanner at the door, a key component of the inventory tracking system.

"You know very well they've never left this place."

Taking Enton's order for a turkey sandwich, Sebastian exited the bookshop, the bell over the door tinkling as he went.

The search went on for hours. Enton discovered sections of the bookshop he'd forgotten existed. And in one section — not one he'd forgotten, just one he hadn't visited in ages — he had a flash of memory. It was the very spot they'd built the book fort in the framed photo.

Enton had an idea. It was such a rare thing for him to have ideas, good ones anyway, that for a moment he doubted himself and almost went back to searching. Instead, he dialed Sebastian's number.

"Sebastian?" Enton whispered into his phone.

"Obviously. What's up?"

"When did my grandpa install this book checker thingamajig? I don't remember him having it when I was a kid."

"Well, we've always had strict inventory keeping protocols," Sebastian said, as if talking about a bioengineering lab rather than a bookstore. "But the inventory software and scanner system only went in about a year ago."

"When he started feeling unwell?"

"Yep. Pretty much after the diagnosis. I told him it would be an easy way to keep track of stock for when he passed on the store."

"He was that open with you about his prognosis?" Enton asked with a stab of guilt. He'd only learned Gramps was sick a few weeks before he died.

"We go back a long way."

"You and your family, you mean?" Enton asked, since Sebastian was at least a decade younger than himself. Wasn't he?

"Of course. Anyway, when he first got the system, he entered a couple of numbers to test it out. I'm pretty sure he deleted them when the system went live, though."

But what if he hadn't?

"Thanks, Sebastian."

"No problem. And, Enton?"

"Yeah?"

"The store means a lot to people. I know not to you two. You'd rather have first-class tickets—" Enton wanted to protest, to say he wasn't entirely sure about that, but Sebastian didn't give him time. "But the place, it really is magic. I'm going to say this once and only once." Enton gripped tighter to the phone as it slipped against the cold sweat that had sprouted from his palm. "You will want for nothing if you keep the shop."

"What's that mean? I've seen the ledgers. Gramps wasn't exactly raking it in."

"Your grandfather had everything he wanted.

Except a closer bond to you two, of course. Think about it. He was ill for a year, yet he left behind only the tiniest of medical bills."

"He had Medicare."

Sebastian laughed. "Enton, if you think Medicare would cover even half of those bills, you really need to speak with some senior citizens. We've got plenty who come in. They feel comfortable here. As do their middle-aged children, who practically grew up in the shop and now bring their kids in. It's more than just a bookstore."

"Yeah, well, it doesn't matter," Enton said apologetically. "Reg has this deal all set."

"That's true. Is that all you wanted?"

"Yeah, that's it. Thanks, Sebastian."

Barely five minutes after Enton hung up the phone, Sebastian returned with his sandwich. Enton roamed around the shop, munching through the thick bread and savoring the perfectly roasted turkey accompanied with just the right amount of cranberry sauce.

He aimlessly wandered the stacks of shelves, not bothering to search. There was no point. He was pretty sure what two books were on that record. And he knew he could pretend he didn't have a clue, that he couldn't find the books. If so, the deal would fall through. Reggie would be disappointed, but did that matter compared to the disappointment of a whole neighborhood?

"Damn it!" Reggie shouted from somewhere in the vicinity of the travel section. Enton crammed the rest of the sandwich in his mouth and jogged over as Reggie continued swearing.

"What is it?" Enton asked.

Reggie had been staring at his phone. He turned it to Enton. Under the logo of Reggie's credit card company were the words, '*Credit limit exceeded. Your account has been locked.*'

"Someone hack your account?"

"No, I— Look, I sort of spent more than I should on those ads and signs and stuff. I thought we'd be swimming in dough before any other bills came through. This deal has to happen, Enton."

"I can help pay for the ads."

"It's not just the ads." Reggie shoved the phone in his back pocket, then rubbed the back of his neck. "If there's a breach in contract with the developer, I gotta pay a portion of the sale price, remember?"

"Yeah, but you said it was just a small fee. It's no big deal, right?" Enton couldn't figure out why it suddenly felt like a rhinoceros was marching around inside his belly.

Reggie swallowed hard, then seemed to have trouble meeting his brother's eyes as he muttered, "It's a ten percent penalty fee."

At first, Enton didn't think that was too bad. They'd have to do some clever financing, but surely they'd—

That's when Enton realized he'd been thinking $30,000, one percent of three million. Ten percent was—

His turkey sandwich threatened to come back up... along with the rhinoceros. But then, to Enton's surprise, a sense of resolute certainty filled him and the rhino settled down, possibly to munch on the sandwich.

"Let's go exploring," said Enton.

"We need to find those books," Reggie insisted.

"We will."

"But the scanner thing."

"Is not incorrect."

"Then how did they get on the inventory?"

Enton glanced toward Sebastian, who was dusting a display where the cookbooks had once been. Could Sebastian have—? But that was ridiculous, wasn't it? Sebastian wouldn't have been more than a toddler the last time Enton remembered seeing the books he was certain were the ones in question. Still, Enton couldn't shake the feeling that Sebastian was somehow involved.

Chapter Sixteen

I think books are like people, in the sense
that they'll turn up in your life when you
most need them.

—Emma Thompson

In a far corner of the shop's second level,
Enton tugged on a thick cord to pull down a set of
recessed wooden steps. Enton climbed three of
the narrow risers, then looked back to his brother,
who stood well back, his forehead clammy with
sweat.

"Coming up?" Enton asked, even though he
knew his twin had always had a visceral fear of
what might be lurking in the attic's dimly lit
corners.

Reggie shook his head before the excuse he'd
given since they were kids found its way to his
lips. "You know, I'm not sure I'll fit through that
opening. Besides," he added after handing Enton
a flashlight, "you'll want me here if you need to

hand anything down."

Amused that he could do something his brother couldn't, Enton continued the climb up the remaining risers.

The attic looked the same as he remembered. The space had no real floor, just a few planks of wood that had been placed across the evenly spaced rafters to create a walkway. Despite Reggie's phobia, Enton's only worry up here was making a misstep on one of the dusty planks and falling straight through to the floor below. Which is why he didn't move at first. He took his time to scan the attic until, at the end of a series of three zigzagging planks, he spotted a cardboard box with *THE BOYS' MEMORABILIA* written on the side in Gramps's blocky handwriting.

Taking mincing steps over the crossbeams, Enton made his way to the box.

"Did you find it yet?" shouted Reggie, startling Enton so hard his left foot slipped off the edge of the plank. Using core muscles he didn't know he possessed, he kept his balance, his toe only grazing the drywall of what was the second floor's ceiling.

"Give me half a minute, will ya?"

Shakily, Enton made it to the box. A cloud of dust puffed up when Enton ripped off the tape holding the flaps shut. Inside, he discovered two teddy bears wearing tiny t-shirts — one embroidered with an E, the other with an R; a photo album; a few record albums by one-hit wonders; a collection of toy cars; and, slipped in so their spines faced up, two slim, hardbound books.

Enton slid them out, then opened the front cover of one. It had been his. A story about an elephant who thought he was a mouse. Written on the inside cover, in the same blocky handwriting as on the box, was a message from his grandfather.

To Enton,
Remember, reading will always support you, unlike the raft this elephant tries to ride.
—Gramps

And below his grandfather's sharp signature was a series of numbers. A chill went through Enton despite the cloying heat of the attic.

Enton then opened Reggie's book — a story of a jalopy who thought it was a race car. On the inner cover, Gramps had written to Reggie, "*Never abandon books. They're your ticket to a first-class life.*"

At the words, gooseflesh sprang up along Enton's arms. And, just as with his elephant book,

Gramps's signature was followed by a string of numbers.

"Enton!"

"Yeah, I got them," Enton said, even though he was tempted to lie. Reggie was too afraid to climb even the first of the wooden steps. If Enton didn't bring these two books down, his twin would never know the key to selling the bookshop was right over their heads.

Sebastian said the store would give them a good life, that they would never want for anything. But Enton couldn't trick his brother. It wasn't right to lie to the only family he had. He brought the books down, tucked under his arm as he descended the stairs.

"You still have the inventory sheet?" Enton asked.

"Why? Those have got to be the books," Reggie said, as excited as an archaeologist who's just found a Saxon hoard. "Aren't they just the loveliest little hunks of tree pulp?"

Reggie grabbed for the books, but Enton pulled them back. Reggie narrowed his eyes at his brother.

"Just humor me. The inventory?"

Reggie dropped his hands, pulled the sheet out of his back pocket, and unfolded it. "Any other requests?"

Enton had recognized the number under Gramps's signature, but he had to be sure. He had to verify the very eerie—

Eerie what? Coincidence? Trick? Magic?

Enton chided himself. Surely, it was just Gramps using a numbering system he'd developed.

"Read the number for this one," Enton said and opened his book. Reggie read out the number. Enton wasn't the least bit surprised that the two numbers were exact matches. "Now yours."

"Mine?"

"The race car one, it's yours. You don't remember it?" Enton asked incredulously, then held the book so Reggie could see the cover. On the jalopy's license plate, Reggie had written his name in a child's jagged and jumbled scrawl.

"Oh, yeah. Man, I loved that book. Remember how I used to read it out loud to you at night?"

"Even when I was trying to go to sleep. Now read the number."

Another exact match.

"What's all this with the numbers?" Reggie asked.

Enton showed his twin the inside covers.

"The ink is the same as the inscriptions. It's also faded just as much. He wrote these numbers decades ago."

For a moment, Reggie's face went slack with confused awe. "What's it mean?"

Enton didn't want to say. He didn't want to tell Reggie he thought something otherworldly was going on. That somehow their grandfather had known the numbers for an inventory system more than thirty years before it even existed. That he thought Sebastian might be—

"It's obvious," Reggie said in the manner of someone who's just struggled through a puzzle, then pretends the solution was obvious from the start. "Gramps got these out of storage when they set up the inventory system, then he manually entered numbers he'd already written."

Enton didn't think this was the case at all. The dust on the box had been thick, far too thick for the box to have been opened only a year ago when the inventory system had been installed.

"But where'd the numbers come from?" prodded Enton.

"Who knows? They're probably just random. Maybe Gramps jotted down numbers like some people doodle. Now, you got a dollar on you?"

"Why?"

"Because you're going to sell me your book and I'll sell you mine. That way, all the inventory on this sheet will have been sold. Clever, huh?"

Enton had to admit it was. They exchanged

books. They exchanged dollars. They even wrote each other receipts for the transactions. Even the lawyer agreed it was all very legal when Reggie called to tell her everything had been settled. Once he sent her a photo of the receipts they'd written, she told them the contingency had been met and she would release the shop's title for the sale.

CHAPTER SEVENTEEN

The best books are those that tell you what
you already know.

—George Orwell

The following morning, as Enton pondered the safety of the milk in their struggling refrigerator, Reggie phoned the developer with the good news. And was immediately put on hold by a secretary who sounded in need of at least three more hours of sleep.

While Reggie waited on hold, he flipped through the elephant book, laughing at the poor thing's attempts to be something he wasn't. Still on hold by the end of the story, he perused the one about the car. Just like the wayward jalopy careening around the raceway, a world of memories raced around Reggie's head.

Flashes of his dad explaining to him the meaning of the word *jalopy*, of his mom telling it was okay to write his name on the license plate on the cover, and of Enton's small snores as Reggie read the book to his twin because he knew it helped his brother sleep.

And then the memory of the day he and Enton had been sprawled across the floor of Gramps's office, reading their books for what must have been the hundredth time.

Gramps had been at his desk. He'd taken a call. Reggie had stopped reading at the strange tone in Gramps's usually chipper voice. But Reggie hadn't dared to look up. Not until Gramps, his knees creaking as he did so, sat cross-legged on the floor with his grandsons and told them their parents had died in a car accident, but that they could live with him as long as they liked.

Other than the ones teachers forced him to read, Reggie never picked up another book from that day forward. He blamed books for his parents' deaths. By the time he was a teenager, he knew that was ridiculous, that books didn't cause a drunk driver to smash into his mom and dad's Toyota, but the idea had not only rooted deep within him, it had also grown.

The shop he'd played in before his parents died, the place where he'd once felt most safe, he came to view as a bastion of doom. He began to hate it, to despise its very presence. He stopped going in to help Gramps after school, and summers became a time for playing baseball, not playing amongst the stacks. And Enton, always willing to go along with his twin, had done likewise.

But the book about the jalopy, the wannabe race car, had hit Reggie harder than he'd expected. Books weren't terrible things. Books were full of life and meaning and joy. And Gramps had spent a lifetime filling his customers', his *friends'*, lives with meaning and joy. The bookshop wasn't a place of doom. It was a place full of new worlds and new possibilities.

* * *

As happy and horrible memories played through Reggie's mind and hold music played in his ear, Enton gave up on the milk and was once again staring intently at the photo of himself and Reggie in their book fort.

What was it about the picture that kept drawing his eye? It reminded him of squinting at an optical illusion and still not seeing the image he was meant to see.

And then Enton tilted his head.

There. In the grey body of the elephant on the cover of his book. A reflection.

Before, Enton had thought it was the flash of a camera, but as he leaned in closer, he could make out dark hair, high cheekbones, mischievous eyes. And now that his face was so close, he made out something else he'd missed. A handle sticking out from behind the fort. The handle of a wagon.

"Reggie!" Enton cried out and spun around.

At the table, phone still pressed to his ear, Reggie sat with the race car book open to the last page. Enton would never bring it up, but he swore he heard his brother sniffle.

"Reg, look at this." Enton pushed the book aside and replaced it with the photo. He pointed at the body of the elephant.

"Yeah, that's your book," Reggie said, his voice hoarse with emotion. "Well, my book now."

"No— Sorry, are you speaking to someone?"

"On hold." Reggie turned the phone so Enton could also enjoy the instrumental rendition of Kenny Loggins's "Footloose".

"No, not the book." Enton tapped his finger on the reflection. "That face. That's Sebastian. Looking the exact same as he does now."

"It's probably his dad," Reggie said dismissively.

"I don't think we should sell the shop." As soon as the words gushed from his lips, Enton couldn't believe he'd said them. He'd been holding in the thought for the past several days, maybe longer. But now he'd finally said it. He'd finally admitted what he wanted and his brother didn't. "I just mean, we— That is—"

Reggie stared at him. Not angrily. Not contemptuously. Not like he was about to chastise Enton for his sentimentality. But — and Enton wasn't entirely sure he believed what he was seeing — like he understood. Like he might almost be coming around to the same conclusion, but hadn't quite gotten there.

"I was," Reggie started, but just then the music stopped. He perked up the way people do when a lengthy hold might have finally reached its end. "Yes, it's Reginald Bookman. The lawyer told you? That's great," Reggie said as if it were anything but great. Enton mentally pleaded with him to cancel the deal, to say they'd changed their minds. But then they'd be in breach of contract, and Enton knew the cost of that could bankrupt them. The unstoppable wheels of real estate had been set in motion. "I understand. You're able to come by to check it over today? Yep, last time I saw it, it was in the same condition." Reggie then gave a phony chuckle. "Of course, minus the books. Good one. Yes. See you at ten."

Reggie said goodbye and hung up the phone. "We're going to be millionaires," he announced with feigned enthusiasm.

"But the shop."

"It's just one bookstore. There's plenty of them in Portland. It's not like we're closing the only hospital in a hundred-mile radius."

"And Sebastian? This photo? What does that mean?"

"Where is your head? It's his dad. It's gotta be, right?" Reggie added, his voice full of doubt and his body hunched like a man forced into a bad decision. "Come on, we better get over there to meet the developer."

They were almost out the door when Enton's phone rang. He glanced at the screen.

"It's Sebastian."

"Ask him how old he is," Reggie scoffed.

Enton answered the call. Even without drinking the possibly sour milk, his stomach clenched.

"Say that again. How bad? Anyone hurt? Never mind, we'll be right there."

Enton jammed the phone back into his pocket.

"Let's go," he said, pushing past Reggie to get out the door as quickly as possible.

"What's going on?" Reggie called after him.

"The bookstore's on fire."

CHAPTER EIGHTEEN

A book is a dream you hold in your hands.

—Neil Gaiman

The scene in front of the shop was unsurprisingly chaotic. Gawkers gawked, police policed, and firefighters, well, they stood around assessing things. The flames had been put out, and the investigators had just finished checking for any signs of arson.

"Looks like some faulty wiring overheated," said the lead fire inspector. "Only thing is, the wiring where the fire started? Some of it looks new. Did you have a security system installed recently?"

Sebastian and Enton turned to Reggie, who was rubbing the back of his neck.

"Well, sure. We were— That's to say, there were some discrepancies with our stock, so I wanted to keep an eye on things. I followed all the instructions on YouTube for the installation," he added hurriedly. "I didn't do anything wrong."

"No one's implying you did, sir," the inspector said. "This happens a lot with older buildings. I've probably responded to fires in most of these shops along here. Never this one, though. Always seemed to escape unscathed." He shrugged. "Guess your luck ran out."

"And the damage?"

"Could have been worse. Plenty of smoke damage, and you'll need to rebuild the corner of the shop where the worst of the fire was, but it looks like you might already have help with that." He tipped his head in the direction of a group of a dozen or so people who were dressed in, of all things, Christmas sweaters and carrying cleaning equipment, repair tools, and cans of paint.

Enton heard a squishy sound from Reggie's throat. Before Reggie could find his voice, a sharp-faced woman in a crisply tailored, navy blue suit was pushing through and ignoring the police insisting she couldn't go beyond the barrier.

"Do you know who I am?" the woman asked.

"No, not really," said the cop dryly.

"I could buy and sell your department in the blink of an eye."

"Could you remodel the break room while you're at it? The lighting in there is awful."

The woman, not appreciating police wit, continued on until she was at Reggie's side.

"What's going on here, Mr Bookman?"

Before Reggie could answer, Sebastian pointed to the firefighters and the big red trucks. "Fire. Either that or someone took my fancy dress invitations far too seriously."

Even Reggie had trouble biting back a smirk as the woman tried to work out if Sebastian was serious.

"There's been a fire here? Is this some sort of scam you're pulling, Mr Bookman? The building must be in its original condition per our contract with you. If it's ruined—"

"It's really only superficial damage, for the most part," assured the fire inspector in the manner of someone trying to be helpful.

"Damaged," the woman said flatly. "So not in the condition when I last viewed it?"

"What's it matter? Aren't you just going to tear it down?" Enton asked.

The woman gave a withering sigh. "It is how we make projects such as this truly profitable for our investors. Designers pay extremely well for these antique interior finishings, but only if they are in pristine condition. You clearly know nothing of real estate development."

"Does it turn you into an insufferable ass, or is that a prerequisite?" asked Sebastian in a tone of genuine interest.

The woman glared at Sebastian a moment, then flicked her gaze away as if the clerk wasn't worth her time. "As to your question," she said, addressing Enton contemptuously, "we will not 'just tear it down'. At the start, we maintain the basic structure of the architecture while modernizing various elements with state-of-the-art design and inspiration so the entire block of units flow and harmonize with the best comfort money can buy. We meld together the most modern domestic art while underpinning it with an old-world charm. Any damage could interfere with our designers' ability to achieve the optimal fluidity of space."

"Didn't get a word of that," said the fire inspector.

Sebastian explained, "It's fancy talk for, 'We're going to gut the place and remove its soul, spend as little as possible to slap up some flimsy new walls, throw a bunch of marketing speak at it, then charge the new tenants scads of money'."

"Yeah, that's what I thought she said."

"Look," Reggie began, "I haven't spoken to my brother about this, but I don't think—"

"No, Mr Bookman, do not try to pull that. The deal was that this place be in the same condition as when the contract was signed." The woman began to open the folder she'd been holding. "Do I need to show proof of the previous condition?"

"No, I was just wondering—"

"Oh, I see how it is. Whatever. I'll play your little game. Because this property is the lynchpin for the project, I'm able to move up the bid from three to four million, but I guarantee you that is our final offer."

Reggie looked to his twin. Enton gave the smallest shake of his head, although he doubted his brother wanted his opinion. Reggie revealed nothing. No sign of agreement or disagreement.

After staring at the smoke-stained windows for several moments, Reggie said, "I have to agree." The woman opened her mouth to speak, but Reggie continued, "The deal was indeed for the shop to be in the same condition as when you first viewed it. It is not in that condition, and while your generous offer is appreciated, as I was trying to say, I don't think we can, in good faith, allow you to make such a deal."

"Okay, fine," the woman said with an impatient sigh. She flicked open her folder and gave the paperwork inside the briefest of glances. "Our designers can sort out the damage. Six million. It's my final offer."

The fire inspector, Sebastian, and Enton all muttered curses of shock and surprise under their breath.

"Really," Reggie said, his voice full of innocence, "I couldn't live with myself. The damage. It could be structural." The fire inspector started to object. Enton pinched his arm to quiet him as Reggie added, "I simply couldn't bear it if someone got hurt."

The woman leaned in. "This is the keystone to this development project. If you ruin this for me, I will ruin you. Or are you somehow able to afford that breach of contract fee?" When Reggie's only response was to swallow the lump in his throat, the woman smirked and said, "I'm glad we've come to an understanding."

"Actually," said the lawyer, striding up with a broad grin on her face, "I've been looking over Mr Bookman's contract with you, and it appears you've forgotten about clause fifteen."

CHAPTER NINETEEN

Books are the plane, and the train, and the
road. They are the destination and the
journey. They are home.

—Anna Quindlen

"Clause fifteen? That was supposed to have
been—" The developer, whose haughty air had
momentarily deflated, fought to refill her balloon
of self-importance. "That is...which clause do you
mean?"

"Oh, you know the one," the lawyer said
chummily. "The clause with the loophole. The one
that states if the building isn't in the same
condition as when the contract was made,
regardless of the cause, all aspects of the contract
are invalid. I have all sorts of speculations about
why that clause is in there, but as it stands, if you
wanted to buy the property in this state, a whole
new set of documents would have to be drawn
up. Mr Bookman, are you still interested in

pursuing that course of action?"

Reggie stared at her, once more unable to speak.

"She means, do you still want to make a deal with this well-dressed weasel?" Sebastian whispered to him.

"I know what she means. And she's right. If my brother feels the same, of course." Reggie looked to his twin. Enton nodded his agreement. "Then yes, we'd like to consider the contract invalid."

"Better luck destroying the character of a neighborhood some other time," Sebastian said as he waggled his fingers at the developer, who spun around and stormed off. After tripping over one of the fire hoses.

"What a twat," the fire inspector said, and everyone agreed with his assessment.

"That was some good work," Enton said to the lawyer. "Thank you."

Sheepishly, Reggie then asked, "When you said all aspects of the deal were invalid, does that include the fee for breach of contract?"

"It's always possible they could push for it on a technicality." Sweat broke out across Reggie's prominent forehead. Fearing he might pass out, the lawyer rushed to reassure him. "But I doubt they will. Not unless the developer wants me to start digging into the real reason that clause is included in any of their contracts. No one's been gutsy enough to fight them yet, but there have been complaints about them over the years.

"See, this developer strikes quick and locks sellers into a contract before sending out feelers to potential investors. Then, if they discover no one's interested in investing in the property acquisition, they 'accidentally' break off a piece of molding or spill tomato juice on the carpeting and declare the deal's off per clause fifteen. I'm honestly surprised they're still trying to pull that same old trick. Anyway, I'm just glad you sent me a copy of the contract to look over."

"But I didn't—" Reggie began, then scrunched up his face as he tried to remember whether he had sent over the contract or not. Enton glanced at Sebastian, and rather than feeling annoyed at the clerk's telling grin, Enton felt a warm surge of gratitude. He wanted to hug the clerk, but instead, he merely thanked the lawyer again.

"Glad to see my talents in contract law aren't going to waste," the lawyer said. "So, you're staying in the book business?"

Reggie gave a shrug of defeat, but Enton didn't miss the faintest hint of a smile and a light in his brother's eyes he hadn't seen in years.

"Looks like it," Enton replied.

"Even though you have no books?"

"I'm sure we'll be able to restock in no time,"

said Sebastian.

Reggie then stepped forward and addressed the people carrying mops, paint cans, and power tools.

"We got some things to sort out before you can help, but—" Enton didn't miss the hitch in his brother's throat "—but thank you. We'll let you know when we need you."

With the fire inspector's permission, Enton, Reggie, and Sebastian went in to assess the worst of the damage. The children's section, the corner of the shop where the brothers had built their book fort all those years ago, was now a sodden mess. The floorboards and drywall were singed and blackened, and the chairs had collapsed into soggy stuffing and charred kindling.

"Well, thanks to your recent sales and donations, at least no books got ruined," said Sebastian wryly. "Should we start cleaning up?"

"We probably need to wait for an insurance adjuster or something, don't we?" said Enton, wondering how they would pay for the cleanup and remodeling. Sure, there was insurance, and at least the looming fear of that breach of contract fee was gone, but there was still all the debt Reggie had racked up with the ads and flyers and who knew what else. Unable to stop himself, Enton groaned.

"Maybe you should go out and get the details from your lawyer," suggested Sebastian, practically shooing the brothers out of their own shop. "And grab me a coffee while you're out there."

The fire inspector, who'd been amiably chatting with the lawyer when the Bookman brothers came out, had dealt with the process enough to advise them that basic cleanup could begin any time they were ready, since all the details of the damage were already in his report.

"The damp's going to be your worst problem," he told them. "Trust me, the sooner you start drying things out, the better."

The lawyer then volunteered to phone the insurance company for them since they probably had other things on their minds.

"So you can tally up more billable hours?" Reggie asked.

"No, because I want to help. This place holds a lot of memories for me. I'd be lying if I said a battered copy of Grisham's first novel didn't inspire me to study law. Funny, though. I don't even remember putting it in my basket. I was convinced I wanted to be an astronomer and had been perusing books on the solar system. Hadn't even been in the fiction section. Then, when I checked out, there it was, the Grisham. I figured for twenty-five cents, why not. And even though I swear that cover was half falling off when the clerk dropped it in my bag, when I got home it looked brand new. Weird, huh? Must've been the lighting. Anyway, I better go now. I'll call you as soon as I have more information."

The fire inspector walked with her, and before they were out of Enton's line of sight, he saw the lawyer jot down her number on a business card and hand it to the now-grinning inspector.

"We better get Sebastian his coffee," Reggie said. "I could use some caffeine myself."

The gawkers had worked up a thirst, so the line at the coffee shop was out the door. But Reggie and Enton waited, unaware of the time as they pondered what to do next.

"Sebastian said the shop would provide for us," Enton said when they were only two customers away from the order counter. "What do you think he meant?"

"I think he just likes to hear himself talk."

"Gramps never seemed to want for anything."

"Different generation. He didn't have the same cravings as us."

"Still—"

"Next," called the barista, and Reggie and Enton placed their orders. Just then, the espresso machine clogged up and it took fifteen minutes for it to start sputtering again. Their feet aching from standing so long, the brothers finally collected their orders and headed back to the bookstore.

CHAPTER TWENTY

The library is inhabited by spirits that
come out of the pages at night.

—Isabel Allende

Once back inside the shop, Enton sniffed. He could smell the coffee in his hand, but there was no stench of smoke, burnt carpet, or sodden ashes. He and Reggie made their way back to the store's damaged area. The area that had been a charred disaster only an hour ago now showed no sign of the fire other than a large fan oscillating its breeze over the damp flooring.

Enton looked around. It had been a strange and stress-filled day, and of course, the shop looked different with no books. Maybe they'd walked to the wrong section.

"Ah, just what I needed," said Sebastian, who took the coffee from Enton's hand, as if he knew exactly which cup was meant for him.

"What happened to the mess?" asked Enton.

"Damage wasn't as bad as all that. Everyone knows the worst bit is the damp. Once I got the fans going, the rest practically fixed itself."

"But there was standing water," said Reggie. "We weren't gone *that* long."

"Elbow grease." Sebastian shrugged and sipped his coffee.

"I don't believe you," said Enton. "Something's not right about you." Sebastian made a show of checking his limbs. "Not physically. You're in a picture of us from thirty years ago. And in it, you look just like you do now."

"It's his dad," Reggie insisted, but Enton stared challengingly at Sebastian.

"What are you?" Enton asked, feeling both foolish and confidently curious. "Fairy? Elf? Wizard?"

"Oh, good lord," Reggie muttered and shook his head.

"Your brother," Sebastian said to Enton while pointing at Reggie, "nailed it on the head. Lord Sebastian, at your service. Don't worry, you don't have to bow."

"You're a lord?" Enton stated hesitantly.

Sebastian, in the midst of taking another sip of his drink, nodded. "It's not technically correct, but *Lord Sebastian* flows off the tongue better than *Local Demigod and Guardian Presence Sebastian.*

But we've gotten off our ceremonial high horses in the past century, so just Sebastian is fine."

"Wait, what?" Reggie stammered. "*We*?"

"Sure. All places have a... I don't know, a spirit, shall we say. For the past eighty years, I happen to be the one for this shop. However, I can tell you I wasn't thrilled when Darius moved in next door—"

"Darius?" interrupted Enton, utterly bewildered since he knew very well that the baker's name was Sylvester, and the woman who ran the pet shop was called Petra.

"Darius, yes. The local demigod of the bakery. In 1066, we got in a little tiff over— Well, I no longer recall, but we haven't gotten along since. Sometimes you can't pick your neighbors, can you?"

"And what exactly do you do?" asked Enton, since Reggie seemed to have lost the ability to speak.

"We make sure places thrive, that they stay safe, that their owners are taken care of. When we adopt a domain, it retains its independence and authenticity, and people find themselves inexplicably drawn to it. I can see the next question bubbling in that mind of yours. Why a bookstore?" Enton nodded. "I've always had an affinity for books. I've protected the workshops of scribes, I've guided the hands of monks in their scriptorium, I've helped safeguard libraries. Not the one in Alexandria," Sebastian added scathingly. "I'm still not speaking to Una for leaving her post that day and letting the place burn down. I mean, of all the idiotic— Sorry," Sebastian raised a hand to stop himself. "All these centuries later, and the wound is still raw."

"So you've always been here?" Enton asked.

"Since the first book was stocked on the shelves, I was immediately drawn here. Your grandfather was my favorite owner to work with, and I was doing a pretty good job of things until you two took over."

"Did Gramps know? About you?"

"Hard to miss that your only employee never ages and can work all hours without complaint."

"You. Protect," Reggie said slowly, as if re-learning how to form words. "All the trouble we had selling the books. That was because of you?"

"Guilty," Sebastian beamed.

When his brother lifted his arms, Enton thought Reggie was preparing to punch Sebastian. Reggie then lunged forward before Enton could stop him. But instead of a fist to Sebastian's face, Reggie's arms wrapped around the clerk who had just, in the very second before the embrace, set down his coffee.

"Thank you," Reggie said, then stepped out of the hug.

"Any time. Now, shall we fill these shelves?"

"With what?" Reggie asked. "The only two books we still own?"

"We might be able to dig up a few more. Sabrina," Sebastian shouted in the direction of the shop's entrance.

And in walked the dark-haired girl despite Enton swearing he'd locked the door when they'd entered the shop after returning from getting coffee. Behind her, she pulled her wagon. She meandered her way through the store, with books appearing on the shelves as she passed them by. The books lined up neatly by genre, and arranged themselves in precise alphabetical order.

"What the—?" Enton began. He'd suspected something was unique about Sebastian. In fact, he'd barely been surprised by what the clerk had revealed about himself, but this went far beyond Enton's realm of imagination. "How?"

"Something to do with the wagon," said Sebastian. "I honestly don't know how she does it, and being a stubborn old mule, my sister refuses to divulge her secrets." The clerk paused to scowl mockingly at the girl, who responded by adding a flippant bounce to her step. "Sabrina's a demigod of plenty. I don't know if it's genetic or just coincidence, but we both seem to have developed a love of the written word. So, wherever she goes and wherever they're needed or wanted, books appear."

Enton watched. Amazed and delighted. If he squinted his eyes and angled his head just right, he could indeed detect shapes, like the faded images of books, stacked on the wagon. As Sabrina strolled along, the shapes floated up from the wagon and became solid when they took their places on a shelf.

"They only appear solid," said Sebastian, as if reading Enton's thoughts. "They'll still shift and change and become just what somebody was looking for when needed. In truth, only once a person begins reading it does a book finally become real."

"But this is—" Enton said, full of wonder. "I mean, this is next-level sorcery."

"Not sorcery. Magic. Books are magic." Sebastian gestured to the sign above the entryway. "That magic is part of what we rule over, what we gather our own energy from. Books are so much more than the pulp of dead trees and some ink. Books have a life of their own, they have an essence, they affect people's hearts and minds, and part of my job is seeing that readers find the exact book they need precisely when they need it. And while my work happens in this shop, Sabrina enjoys getting out and about. You've seen her roaming through the neighborhoods."

Enton and Reggie said they had.

"Well, as she goes along, she collects the essence of books that have already been read or ones that have been long forgotten. She then brings all those essences here to give them a new life. Of course, it's not all magical; you still get stock the old-fashioned way — orders for new releases, buybacks of used books, that sort of thing. Now, it's been quite the day. Why don't you two go home? We'll get things ready for the grand reopening in, say, a couple weeks?"

"Why not tomorrow?" Enton asked eagerly.

"Because no one's going to believe you fixed the place up, dried out the carpeting, and restocked the shelves overnight. So, go home, enjoy yourselves, and," he said, lifting his cup, "thanks for the coffee."

CHAPTER TWENTY-ONE

Books may well be the only true magic.

—Alice Hoffman

Reggie and Enton left the shop. Since Reggie was still in half a daze and probably shouldn't be behind the wheel, Enton drove them home.

Then Enton wondered about his own mental state as he cruised right past their house, only realizing his mistake when he reached the end of the block and had to loop back around. As he pulled up to their humble abode, he understood why he'd missed it. The place was unrecognizable.

Sure, it was still the same three-bedroom bungalow with an off-center front door and a driveway leading to a detached garage. But other than those basic bits of architecture, Enton had to rub his eyes and double check the wooden numbers nailed up beside the door did indeed match their address.

The garden, which had always been a weedy patchwork of barkdust and scrubby grass, was now filled with bright perennials and tidily trimmed shrubs. Reggie, apparently still too much in a daze to notice, trailed behind his brother up the newly paved walkway.

When Enton pushed open the freshly painted front door, it didn't creak. Stepping inside, he scooped up the mail and saw that the hardwood floors had a shine to them that certainly hadn't been there that morning, the pictures on the wall leading back to the kitchen had been straightened and dusted, and the kitchen had somehow acquired updated appliances and cabinetry.

Enton dropped the mail on a sturdy, rustic-style table he'd always wanted. Curious, he pulled open the door to the cereal cabinet. Without sticking, it revealed a row of unopened boxes of their favorite cereals. Name-brand stuff. Not a generic label amongst the bunch.

Reggie shuffled in and stopped at the fridge — a new, stainless steel contraption whose cooling mechanism barely made a sound. He stood there, gripping the handle as if he'd forgotten how such things worked.

Needing to regain some sense of normalcy, Enton went back to the mail and opened the letter on top. Since it bore no stamp, Enton assumed it must have been hand-delivered. Only after unfolding the sheet did he discover the letter was for Reggie. It was a personal note from the newspaper's editor, who stated that, in light of the fire (the editor begged Reggie to forgive the pun) and the hardship that would put Reggie under, the entirety of Reggie's advertising bill would be cancelled out.

"Reggie, did—?"

"Who did all this?" Reggie muttered, finally looking around the kitchen. His hand still gripped the refrigerator's handle.

Enton, however, had set aside Reggie's debt forgiveness letter for a second piece of mail that had caught his eye.

"Reggie, look at this." Enton held up a thick envelope decorated with the silhouette of an airplane on the back flap.

"Probably junk mail."

But Enton opened it anyway. After reading the cover letter over two— no, *three* times, it took him a moment to speak.

"Reggie, this isn't junk mail," Enton said, as his twin finally tugged on the fridge's handle. The sucking sound of the seal breaking was followed by a gasp. Enton, with all sorts of fears of what might be lurking inside, hurried over and peered over Reggie's shoulder.

Inside, there were no severed heads, swarms of wasps, or Tupperware brimming with snakes (Enton may have picked up one too many horror films from the library recently). Instead, on the top shelf, lined up in a neat row, were six bottles of champagne. The good stuff, too. The stuff normally kept under lock and key at the grocery store.

"Open one," Enton said excitedly. "Open one now, Reg."

"Kind of early in the day, isn't it?"

"Not when you've got something to celebrate."

Enton waved the cover letter, again declaring it was definitely not junk mail. Reggie grabbed it from his brother's hand and started reading.

But, like the bubbles foaming their escape from the bottle he'd just uncorked, Enton couldn't contain himself. "It's two first-class tickets!"

"It's gotta be a scam."

Reggie scrutinized the letter, the itinerary, and the two tickets.

Two tickets that weren't a scam.

Two tickets that would take the Bookman brothers on a privately guided, first-class trip that began with a tour of France's Champagne region and that included free-flowing tastings at the finest producers.

Two tickets for a vacation that would leave the

next day and last two weeks, getting the brothers back just in time for the grand reopening of Bookman's Bookshop.

Two tickets that finally made Reggie Bookman understand what Enton, and their grandfather, had known all along: Books really were magic.

TELEVISION AND MOUSE HUNTING

THE STORY BEHIND THE BOOKMAN BROTHERS

Thank you so much for reading this fanciful tale about the marvels of books.

Obviously, this story makes clear my book addiction and my inability to stop myself from sneaking in a bit of magic to any situation, but where did the roots of this story come from?

Television.

More specifically, a television ad.

Hardly the most inspiring things, right?

And what's even worse... it was a super sappy holiday ad (as if there's any other kind of holiday ad).

In the commercial, a bookshop has just had a fire. The community is devastated, the shop owners are wondering what to do. Meanwhile, throughout the ad, we see the community banding together to rebuild the shop, and we see a little girl going around the neighborhood with a wagon. At the end of the commercial, we discover the girl has gone around collecting books to help restart the bookshop. Hoorah!

Told you it was sappy.

Of course, my warped brain starts thinking, "What if the shop owners realized their book business wasn't profitable? What if they intentionally burnt the place down in the hopes of collecting the insurance money so they could hightail it to the Bahamas? Then this stupid, wagon-toting brat comes along and ropes them into re-opening the shop they hate?"

What can I say? I can only tolerate sappy Christmas ads if I can give them my own twist.

Anyway, this idea kept nagging at me about someone having a bookshop they didn't want, of trying to get rid of it in any way possible, and failing at every attempt. And of course, there had to be a girl with a wagon full of books.

An outline quickly formed.

Then I had to do some "research".

See, the situation I'd come up with — two brothers inheriting a place that could be a potential windfall if not for some "force" preventing them from selling — reminded me of the movie *Mousehunt* with Nathan Lane, Lee Evans, and Christopher Walken (possibly his finest role, in my opinion). Not entirely, because that movie is pure slapstick genius, but enough that I had to watch the movie again.

You know, for research.

I took a few notes while watching the film... and never looked at the notes again. But I did learn that the movie's humor still holds up and I highly recommend it if you need a laugh.

Anyway, movies and television aside....

I hope this novella spoke to your book-loving heart and that you had as much delight in reading it as I did in writing it.

Also, if you'd like another humorous story from me about the love of books, you can get one for free by joining my monthly newsletter* which is full of all kinds of bookish goodies... and cat photos.

If you're interested, go ahead and sign up at the link below...

www.subscribepage.com/ mrsmorris

—Tammie Painter, February 2023

* Don't worry, if it turns out you don't like the newsletter, you can unsubscribe at any time.

If You Enjoyed This Story
The Part Where I Beg for a Review

You may think your opinion doesn't matter, but believe me, it does…at least as far as this book is concerned. I can't guarantee it mattering in any other aspect of your life. Sorry.

See, reviews are vital to help indie authors (like me) get the word out about their books.

Your kind words not only let other readers know this book is worth spending their hard-earned money and valuable reading time on, but are a vital component for me to join in on some pretty influential promotional opportunities.

Basically, you're a superhero who can help launch Enton and Reggie into stardom!

I know! You're feeling pretty powerful, aren't you?

Well, don't waste that power trip. Head over to your favorite book retailer, Goodreads, and/or Bookbub and share a sentence or two (or more, if you're ambitious). Even a star rating would be appreciated.

And if you could tell just one other person about this tale, your superhero powers will absolutely skyrocket.

Thanks!!

ABOUT THE AUTHOR

THAT'S ME...TAMMIE PAINTER

Many moons ago I was a scientist in a neuroscience lab where I got to play with brains and illegal drugs. Now, I'm an award-winning author who turns wickedly strong tea into imaginative fiction (so, basically still playing with brains and drugs).

My fascination for myths, history, and how they interweave inspired my flagship series, The Osteria Chronicles, and my second series, Domna.

But that all got a bit too serious for someone with a strange sense of humor and odd way of looking at the world. So, while waiting for my grandmother's funeral to begin, my brain came up with an idea for a contemporary fantasy trilogy that would be filled with magic, mystery, snarky humor, and the dead who just won't stay dead. That idea turned into The Cassie Black Trilogy.

In my latest series, The Circus of Unusual Creatures, I'm having a great time playing with mythical beasts, sleuthing dragons, and humor-laced mysteries.

When I'm not creating worlds or killing off characters, I can be found gardening, planning my next travel adventure, working as an unpaid servant to three cats and two guinea pigs, or concocting some sort of mess in my kitchen.

You can learn more at *TammiePainter.com*

ALSO BY TAMMIE PAINTER

THE CASSIE BLACK TRILOGY

Work at a funeral home can be mundane. Until you start accidentally bringing the dead to life.

If you like contemporary fantasy with snarky humor, unforgettable characters, piles of pastries, and a little paranormal mystery, you'll find it hard to pry yourself away from the Cassie Black Trilogy...a fish-out-of-water tale that takes you from the streets of Portland to the Tower of London.

The Undead Mr. Tenpenny, The Uncanny Raven Winston, The Untangled Cassie Black

THE OSTERIA CHRONICLES

Myths and heroes may be reborn, but the whims of the gods never change.

Perfect for fans of the mythological adventure of *Clash of the Titans* and *300*, as well as historical fantasy fiction by Madeline Miller and David Gemmel, the Osteria Chronicles are a captivating fantasy series in which the myths, gods, and heroes of Ancient Greece come to life as you've never seen them before.

The Trials of Hercules, The Voyage of Heroes, The Maze of Minos, The Bonds of Osteria, The Battle of Ares, The Return of Odysseus

THE CIRCUS OF UNUSUAL CREATURES

It's not every day you meet an amateur sleuth with fangs.

If you like paranormal, cozy mysteries that mix in laughs in with murderous mayhem and mythical beasts, you'll love The Circus of Unusual Creatures.

Hoard It All Before, Tipping the Scales, Fangs a Million

DOMNA

Destiny isn't given. It's made by cunning, endurance, and, at times, bloodshed.

If you like the political intrigue, adventure, and love triangles of historical fiction by Philippa Gregory and Bernard Cornwell, or the mythological world-building of fantasy fiction by Madeline Miller and Simon Scarrow, you'll love this compelling story of desire, betrayal and rivalry.

AND MORE...

To see and sample my currently available books and stories, just scan the QR code or visit books.bookfunnel.com/ tammiepainterbooks

Let's Stay In Touch!

My Next Book is Coming Soon...

In fact, it might already be here, and there's probably been loads of exciting stuff you've missed out on. You know, like photos of my cats.

Anyway, I love getting to know my readers, so if you'd like to...

- Keep up-to-date with my writing news,
- Chat with me about books you love (and maybe those you hate),
- Receive a free short story or exclusive discount now and then,
- And be among the first to learn about my new releases

...then please do sign up for my monthly newsletter.

As a thank you for signing up, you'll get my short story *Mrs. Morris Meets Death* — a humorously, death-defying tale of time management, mistaken identities, cruise ships.... and romance novels.

Join in on the fun today by scanning this QR code or by heading to *www.subscribepage.com/mrsmorris*

Printed in Great Britain
by Amazon